IN THE BEGGARLY STYLE OF IMITATION
(BELOW THE LEVEL OF CONSCIOUSNESS)

a blewointment book

IN THE BEGGARLY STYLE OF IMITATION

(Below the Level of Consciousness)

JEAN MARC AH-SEN

NIGHTWOOD EDITIONS

2020

Nightwood Editions
P.O. Box 1779
Gibsons, BC VON 1V0
Canada
www.nightwoodeditions.com

COVER DESIGN: Charlotte Gray
COVER PHOTO: Ally Schmaling
COVER MODEL: Kitty Collins
TYPOGRAPHY: Carleton Wilson

Nightwood Editions acknowledges the support of the Canada Council for the Arts, the
Government of Canada, and the Province of British Columbia through the BC Arts Council.

This book has been produced on 100% post-consumer recycled, ancient-forest-free paper,
processed chlorine-free and printed with vegetable-based dyes.

Printed and bound in Canada.

LIBRARY AND ARCHIVES CANADA CATALOGUING IN PUBLICATION

Title: In the beggary style of imitation / Jean Marc Ah-Sen.
Names: Ah-Sen, Jean Marc, 1987- author.
Description: Short stories.
Identifiers: Canadiana (print) 20190201355 | Canadiana (ebook) 20190201398 |
ISBN 9780889713727 (softcover) | ISBN 9780889713734 (ebook)
Classification: LCC PS8601.H2 I5 2020 | DDC C813/.6—dc23

for HULOT

Contents

"What you want is buried in the present tense
Blind alleyways allay the jewels"

–Vic Godard

An Introduction to: *Adamant Deathward Aloofness*

Jean Marc Ah-Sen was born in East York, Toronto in 1987 to two Mauritian emigrés: a gas station attendant and a secretary. He grew up in a multilingual home where French, English and *kreol morisyen* intermingled like bad weather. His upbringing was reportedly "odd" (he was discouraged from being left-handed for fear that using a North American gearshift with the weaker hand would cause difficulty), tinged with "poor moral hygiene" and the kind of insipid regrets that are part and parcel of an adolescence mired in itinerancy. He failed a fledgling career as a cartoonist, largely due to lack of application and an inability to overcome shortcomings in his linework. He transitioned into writing soon after reading a copy of Blaise Cendrars' *Planus* that he had stolen from a schoolmate. Various lacklustre professions supported his early forays into writing, including time spent as a bartender, janitor, office clerk, furniture assembler and debt collector. The name "Ah-Sen" was adopted a half-century earlier by his grandfather, a deserter in Mao's People's Liberation Army who arriving in Africa, secured papers to a new identity.

Ah-Sen has authored a total of ten novels, of which two have seen publication. He considers himself retired from writing. Publication of the eight remaining books, which include *Parametrics of Purity*, *Kilworthy Tanner* and *Mystic Minder*, remain a drawn-out "administrative formality." The better part of his life has been spent rewriting these books, often under my supervision and endorsement. Describing his writing process as an exertion of "Translassitude," or of a "speeding bullet of thought impacting against a wall of adamant, deathward aloofness," encapsulated his lifelong struggle with recording the immediacy of his ideas with the nonchalance of changing out of wet clothes.

Translassitude was the name given to the brief literary movement we founded together to solve this generic problem: how can writers cultivate a phenomenological sensitivity to the world, and turn that material data into works of cultural and artistic relevance? Was there a way to expedite this transmutative process and make it a less arduous task? Translassitude's reason for being was to standardize the logistics of inspiration, which we attempted by marrying my obsessive practice of rewriting existing novels palimpsestically—a practice I called "kilworthying"—with Ah-Sen's theories that the most productive writing periods resulted from self-induced bouts of lassitude and physical exhaustion. It was our belief that the rigours of this literary science produced altered states of consciousness which had definable poetic corollaries.

These states were given the designations of: *omnilassitude, paralassitude, hyperlassitude* and *somnilassitude,* the last of which purportedly allowed its bearer to write books in a state of advanced torpor (and in some exceptional instances, while asleep). Omnilassitude coincided with the dawning impulse to write Translassic literature; paralassitude with the establishment of its themes, images and subtextual possibilities; hyperlassitude with the emergence of a fixed style that systematically governed and enhanced the disparate narrative elements; and somnilassitude with the adoption of a metatextual awareness of this collective process known as Translassitude.

The bad reputation Translassists endured did not end with accusations of the absurdity of these labours; we also became notorious for our employment of two techniques in particular: "draffsacking" and "tuyèring." Draffsacking was a form of collaborative doctoring whereby a lead author composed topic and concluding sentences of all the paragraphs that comprised a text, while a "draffsacker" or secondary author filled in the necessary details under the administration of the lead. The most well-known books written using this technique were Ah-Sen's baroque pseudohistory of the Mauritian Sous Gang, the *nouveau roman Grand Menteur*, and my *causerie*-novel *Sugarelly*.

Tuyèring was the Translassic method of organizing plots in such a manner that the text was permitted to breathe, expanding under the influence of the most ephemeral of structural substances. No outlines were ever used, but a "winch chapter" would be composed psychographically. This chapter could be placed anywhere in the text, so long as it became the *primum movens* of the work in question, the fulcrum along which the entire book would pivot, expand, contract. As successive chapters were written (always deferring to the preceptive logic of the winch chapter), a natural momentum and structure would emerge, allowing the novel to take shape and reveal itself. Ah-Sen almost exclusively wrote winch chapters meant to be situated at the beginning of novels, and had a prodigious archive of over fifty undeveloped winches, some of which are published in this collection ("Underside of Love," "The Slump," "As to Birdlime," "The Lost Norman").

In the Beggarly Style of Imitation (*Below the Level of Consciousness*) is perhaps the purest expression of this tottering and ultimately unsustainable model of creative behaviour. The conceit was simple, but no less hubristic: a miscellany that would reflect the storied genesis and formalization of elements that would become recognized as the modern novel. It was meant to be a celebration of the grand project of writing in its myriad forms—a modern day feuilleton. Unfortunately, the book luxuriates in its failure of this gargantuan task, in the inability of the project ever reaching completion. Quite noticeably, Gothic romances, parables, travelogues and the various forms of bucolic narratives, to name but a few formative examples, are all absent from it (there was some talk of stopping these obvious lacunae by publishing future collections of recitative imitation, but indolence, or I should say *retirement*, proved too attractive). Participating in the musical tradition of the *contrafactum*, in substituting new lyrical content over historical melodies in deliberate acts of textual erasure, however partial and given to reflecting its chronological record, *Imitation* uses familiarity with narrative forms as the basis to produce startling and at other times inefficacious results. The stories on offer are "exercises of stylistic decadence," experiments in bald or disruptive imitation known as the "parametrics of purity."

Imitation had an exploratory mandate, and was perhaps never meant for publication. It was an apprenticeship in writercraft and tropology; or to continue the musical analogy, many of these stories were attempts to "detune" and perform the pieces in an altered key. From a practical standpoint, Ah-Sen and I were simply attempting to understand what artistic results came about from the "hermeneutic square," the four states of Translassic consciousness. But I see now that the project took on new dimensions when Ah-Sen and I decided to dissolve our romantic and professional relationship: not content to rest on

its laurels, it appears the text morphed violently into a meditation on *eros* and its accompanying agonies and delusions, and
perhaps even more unfalteringly, must now also satisfy a tertiary
objective of being an experimental sequel to *Grand Menteur*.

Planned as a trilogy of metaobject codex-novels, *Grand
Menteur*, *In the Beggarly Style of Imitation* and the unreleased
third Menteur book were, in an act of vicious paradox, conceived as diegetic artefacts of dubious authorship ostensibly
written by the subjects of these books themselves, loosed onto
the supra-fictional, real world. These codices were effectively
Walserian microscripts that Sous gang members created to keep
their alibis consistent in the event of capture. The third novel
dealt primarily with the daughters of the Grand Menteur and
Grand Piqûre being asked to record a soundtrack for a stalled
film about the Sous Gang, a kind of gonzo, demon-laden *Day
for Night* directed by Claude Ste. Croix VII and Aldegonde Ste.
Croix VI (a prelude to these events occurs in "Sous Spectacle
Cinema Research Consultation with Bart Testa," while the Ste.
Croix family history is touched on in "As to Birdlime").

A short survey through the stories that follow might not
be inopportune, given Ah-Sen's refusal to go into illustrative
detail about process or organizational reasoning to anyone but
members of the Translassic Society (besides being a fanatically
devoted believer in the intentional fallacy, when pressed publicly on professional ambitions, he would usually offer nothing
more than boffolas about having obscenity laws brought back
on his account).

"Underside of Love" takes place shortly after the events of
Grand Menteur, and prominently features Cherelle Darwish,
the self-effacing, pigeon-hearted daughter of the Grand Piqûre,

the Black Derwish. Readers will recall that Cherelle excelled at receding in the background of the pages of that novel, except when it came to the critical moment of palming off psychotropic mushrooms to Rhonda "Roundelay" Mayacou, the Menteur's daughter. In "Underside," Cherelle is given agency not hitherto afforded by penurious attempts at her characterization, the hysterical nimieties of the preceding novel reduced to the emotional rubble of a melodrama (or perhaps a Semprún novel).

This winch chapter was commissioned by Ah-Sen's friend, the writer Paul Barrett, for a magazine celebrating the career of Barbadian author Austin Clarke. It was a work of parallel fiction that mirrored "Give Us This Day: And Forgive Us" from Clarke's story collection *When He Was Free and Young and He Used to Wear Silks*, borrowing its basic plot elements of a doomed romantic couple, an eviction (and the psychological effects deriving therefrom), and a character uninterested in political activity and metamotivation because their basic needs had yet to be realized. Imitation here served a generative purpose, and was an early incursion into the possibility of two texts operating diachronically as sister stories.

The experiments with overwriting continued with the Borges-inspired "Ah-Sen and I," a palimpsest of "Borges and I" (down to the word count) that even incorporated Ah-Sen's first negative book review. The miming of Henry Fielding's picaresques in "As to Birdlime," which borrows its title from a passage in *Jonathan Wild*, is perhaps the most unabashedly imitative story in the collection, bordering on being a derivative copy; but notwithstanding the most waspish aesthete's choplogic about the pre-eminence of "authentic" literature, surely Ah-Sen cannot be at fault for taking the counsel to walk before running under advisement. These exercises arose at my behest, after all; Ah-Sen's technical fluency with kilworthying was nil, and I believed that rewriting existing passages from writers we admired would eliminate more lame misadventures in composition. Kilworthying was as close to a scientific measure of "sinking into the mind" of an author possible, of becoming intimately familiar with the syntax, grammar and styling that governed their minds. In this fashion, we would be able to trace inspiration to a homologous source, and in so doing, perpetually have ideas at one's elbow.

"Sentiments and Directions from an Unappreciated Contrarian Writer's Widow" and "Swiddenworld: Selected Correspondence with Tabitha Gotlieb-Ryder" are notable not only for working with established forms of the aphoristic and epistolary modes made well-known by writers like La Rochefoucauld, Lichtenberg, Tobias Smollett and Mary Hays, but for furthering the connective nodes with the world of Mauritian Menteurism the most aggressively out of all the installments in *Imitation* after "Underside." "Swiddenworld," taking its cues from James Joyce's letters to Nora Barnacle, accounts for the Menteur's disappearance from his daughter's life, perhaps the greatest unanswered question from *Grand Menteur*, while "Sentiments and Directions" contains Cherelle's meditations on love and loss which resulted from the glossed-over dissolution of her marriage in "Underside."

The lyrics to three of the Black Derwish's Mauritian singles ("Mahebourg," "Triolet," and "Baie-du-Tombeau") panegyrizes and further cements Cherelle's unflinching allegiance to her father's criminal enterprises, while the excerpt from "The Lost Norman" represents the briefest of rapprochements between

the Menteur and the Piqûre, who penned the Norman Wisdom–inspired story together about their favourite English film
star's lost picture. In actuality, this winch chapter existed briefly
as one of the ten novels Ah-Sen had completed, but the majority of the manuscript had been lost in a house fire where it had
been improperly stored. The novel attempted to integrate all the
Norman Wisdom films in an irresolute act of intertextuality,
presenting the filmic Normans as fifteen brothers masquerading
as one man for tax evasion purposes. The book was a damning
condemnation of housing worries, landholdings fraud and can-
tillating landlords who liked to hide their wealth behind Rupert
Rigsby-esque self-flagellation. The book was not particularly
known for its subtlety among those privy to early drafts—if I
am remembering correctly, the book histrionically opened with
the line, "Beneficed scum-legion of the world, thy name is Land-
lord!" *The Lost Norman* was subsequently abandoned, and the
segment here is all that remains of the project.

"The Slump" poses a much more difficult case of account-
ing. I had not read this story until I was given proofs of this collection in preparation for writing these introductory remarks.
It is a legitimate piece of juvenilia dating back to a decade ago
when Ah-Sen began writing in earnest. All I can venture here
is a vague recollection of plans for Cherelle to become a failed
novelist, so it would not be incongruous to suppose that the
story exists, along with "Sentiments and Directions," as one of
Cherelle's earliest literary offerings, and a middling specimen of
vanity at that (*Imitation* is *her* codex, after all).

The greatest artistic liberty on offer is undoubtedly the
inclusion of "A Defence of Misanthropy," which was published
originally in a Translassic encyclical and drafted by my own

hand after kilworthying a William Hazlitt essay. It is also attributed to Cherelle Darwish and perhaps accounts in greater detail for the psychological frame of mind she was in after divorcing her husband and separating from Roderick Borgloon. As anyone can well imagine, all these years onwards the piece appalls me, though I cannot help but marvel at Ah-Sen's complete abandonment of any kind of ethical framework for sourcing found, borrowed and stolen writing to cadge a publishing deal.

It would be a monumental oversight not to mention the fact that *Imitation* had two paramount objectives unrelated to Ah-Sen's literary career: it was meant to publicly lend attention to the Translassic system, but it had to at the same time delegitimize the Sudimentarist school of writing, which encouraged writers to assume the lives of their fictional characters. Sudimentarism was the chief rival to all of the Translassic Society's efforts for validation among writers. These impediments took the form of legal challenges, infiltration of the Society by intelligencers, and in two confirmed instances, the threat of physical violence towards high-ranking Translassic associates using bound Sudimentarist hardbacks, all under the direction of my father, Artepo Lepoitevin, the founder of Sudimentarism. The war of words between the two camps escalated well past acceptable laws of decorum, which undoubtedly contributed to the droves of disaffiliations on both sides. Ah-Sen may have thrown the first stone and deserves his fair share of responsibility for characterizing my father as a participant in the "bourgeois diffidence that forbade extramarital affairs unless it concerned making love with run-on sentences."

An air of ill-starred futility suffuses my memories of these engagements. It is difficult to feel indignant when the source of your woes has left the surface of the earth. When my father died, the way was clear for Transmentarism—a bizarre amalgam of the two systems forged by Ah-Sen's hand—to take the place previously occupied by its primogenitors. Seemingly having cast off the two main stumbling blocks in his life, Ah-Sen was free to pursue his sesquipedalian campaigns in the "literary underground" unencumbered by such inconsiderable factors as friendship, incorruptibility or sincerity of intention.

If there is any justice in this world, Ah-Sen will read this introduction and be mortified by the unlicensed look behind the iron curtain of his mind in the exact degree I was mortified to see no mention of my name in this windowless tome (unless you count "Tabitha Gotlieb-Ryder," the most unflattering of tributes I could conceive for myself), my sizeable contributions to these pieces annulled by some cack-handed legerdemain. Mortification, as the saying goes, is good for the soul.

Ah-Sen can one day write on these issues and cease his parade of false attributions he has publicly advanced behind a monolithic selfdom of staged worry and mock principles. It made perfect sense when Translassitude was a going concern, and I would likewise take full credit for the novels Ah-Sen draffsacked on my behalf, but those days are long behind us, and I derive no commercial benefit from doltish associations with the past; I see no need why he should either.

I suppose Ah-Sen will have the last laugh, though, a laugh partaking in what Jack London called the "grimness of infallibility." He possesses confirmation that the final "sentiment and direction" I delivered unto him all those years ago in our studio on Ludlow Street was in fact a visionary diagnostic of our times; and while it was meant to be in the spirit of an exhortation, I now see that the suggestion that "there are no new ideas, only unusual ways of forgetting" has become little more than a dispensation to "write" with ungrudging impunity.

–K. Tanner,

NYC, 2020

Underside of Love

MANNERLY STYLE OF ELICITATION

Roderick Borgloon was more of a boor, a fool and a scrounger than was humanly possible, but our separation all these years didn't make him any less my dependent. When we were together, things were horrible for me on account of his masculine remoteness and ability to reduce all the warmth of human contact into a wasted effort. The fact that Roddy knew this and still remained absent in my life in all the ways that mattered crushed my faith in him and put a distance between us that I kept alive. He could be morose, entitled, thunderously opinionated, but also thin-skinned and insecure (when I thought him at his best), nullifying my own expectations as a lover. He liked to complain about everything, the state of the world, the injustices that flung themselves onto the streets and into our paths unblessedly—what a world he painted in his mind, even if only half of it was true. Everything I was taught a man could aspire to, everything that a woman could expect in a romantic equal, found a cracked mirror in our domestic partnership.

Part of my complaisance was due to how much I was told that Roddy's affections were all he could muster on another person's behalf—unimaginable feat of compassion that it was—and that whatever shortcomings were derived from this paucity of feeling, they should not be measured against the virtues of a better person: Borgloon was Borgloon, but indeed he was mine. I would be reminded that it was something to have someone to put up with, to coddle, to turn a blind eye to their tomcatting, to endure his ridicule and act as their only port of call for troubled odysseys.

Roddy wanted to be unhappy in life out of a pure ideal of wretchedness. I didn't find this clarity until much later, when I could deliberate on the matter free from the annihilating influence of his cynicism. I knew that he wasn't interested in bettering himself; he only wanted to have something to hold over you. He was poor, he was passed over, he was overeducated and he never let anyone forget it. He loved to tell the story of how he compared pay stubs with a woman he was living with and asked her how in good conscience she could allow him to pay one red cent to live with her. Sane people push these antipathetic characters away, they maintain an undeluded distance, but over time Borgloon became my only kind of emotional sustenance. I experienced limerence over him, had sense abandon me and carve out hollow desire in its place (it was a sexual awakening for me). I absolutely needed the cheap emotions he could provide at the expense of my self-respect.

The first time I laid eyes on him, my legs nearly gave out—it was a low point, so sue me—but I wasn't dragooned into feeling anything for him until much later. A Wrangler jacket with Wrandam zigzags brushing against a yellow T-shirt that read *Apex Novelties* gave the illusion of substance to his blushing boy's body; ketchup-stained velvet flares flowed over a pair of jodhpurs with soles scrupulously fastened by staples, and a brown rollie usually dangled from his mouth. A vision if you were inclined to see it that way. His snub nose had the effect of rendering his face inert and risible. He had a nice enough set of teeth though, except for this one snaggletooth that conveyed a sinister intention his conversation couldn't honestly come by. A nose you couldn't do anything about, that was just genetics, but hygiene told you everything you needed to know about a person.

When we discovered that both our families lived in Antananarivo, biology took us by the reins. We Darwishes emigrated from Mauritius, the Rabinurs were Malagasy—Roddy took the name Borgloon after the city where he bedded his first white woman. It's hard to describe the feeling of finding another islander when you've spent so much time feeling isolated and alone. When it's a romantic attachment, it's akin to *jouissance*, but cut with paranoia and appalling need. In no time at all, I was rotated among a roster of other doe-eyed women in a cycle of anti-domesticity, non-entanglement, what have you. I was the only non-white woman. You couldn't get Borgloon to commit to anything in his mind not worth committing to, but that was his way and the way of many young men who came before and after him.

Borgloon and I had been engaged in this open arrangement for about eight or nine months when I found out I was with child. I knew I wanted to get rid of it as soon as possible. Having a baby here would take the decision of going back to Pereybere or Antananarivo out of my hands; besides, I was far too young to become a mother. I assumed I would be ploughing a lonely furrow. Roddy did not give me an opportunity to discuss the future before he broke all contact with me like the coward I suspected him to be (double-dyed-in-the-wool, podgy little brute who dashed off whenever life got hard). I don't care how he found out about this little detail but I wouldn't have to look very hard since I could count on my hands the people I told the nature of my predicament—Barbara, Harriet, Sveta; that is, the other women who dabbled in Roddy's affections with me.

I lost the child naturally. I had something called a tubal pregnancy, which saved me the trouble of paying out-of-pocket for an operation. I don't know that I would have been able to get the time off work without getting fired in any event, so this was fortunate for me (in the broad sense). This was not the sticking point. It was the way Roddy went about it that had me at the end of my tether; that for all his high talk about the absence of rectitude among the taskmasters of society, when push came to shove, he was just like every other motherfucker in the world without any sort of class. It's silly how this became the sore spot, more than his pusillanimity. I should probably explain what I mean about Roddy's two-facedness a bit better.

I would run into his associates asking after Roddy all the time; everywhere I went I couldn't avoid someone who knew us formerly as a couple. There was this one dullard named Studholme whom I slept with to get back at Roddy. He used to jingle around with loose change in his pockets so people might think how hard up he was.

"Where's Borgloon? I'm weary-sick, he's got the cure for what ails me."

"Oh, go hang," I'd say.

This was how we first hit it off; I thought I could disabuse the city of Roddy's exaltedness one rut at a time.

Studholme asked me why things ended with Roddy—I became very well-versed in this exercise. People would be dismayed to hear their patron saint of hypocrite scholastics impugned, even after I told them what he did to me. They would go on polishing his pedestal like a *mea culpa* was a slate-cleaner—how altruistic Roddy was, on the beam and working more righteously than anyone else to redress all manner of social ills. If they weren't sleeping with him, they were waiting for his benediction. One night, Studholme was giving it to me a little rougher than usual. He collapsed on top of me and asked if I could recall the last thing Roddy was reading.

Roddy didn't care all that much that Studholme and other maundering pseudo-thinkers looked to him as a means to stiffen their resolve and validate their respective causes. Roddy was no academic, but he was no novitiate either; well-read in his own way but coming at a lot of information second-hand. I had no problem with organizing, but it was hard not to laugh at where the bar was set among this group. Flag-burning, Maoist calisthenics, people's war in the Golden Horseshoe. The Rosedale Marxists were learning how to crawl (to and from their Stutz Blackhawks, I suppose).

For every reason Borgloon gave you to despise him, he also reminded you how brilliant he could be. I would oscillate between opposing poles of feeling. I sometimes experienced his comrades' incredulity at hearing Borgloon and I hailed from Africa, followed by their disappointment in not much more than a look that seemed to say "I wish we knew some *real* Africans." Borgloon made an excellent point about how if we weren't being fetishized for the currency our lives could give their theories, we were being decried—by these deputies taking offence in our honour—for losing our roots in the unnavigable canyons of the white world. It was but a handsel of Borgloon's insight and I fell a little in love with him after he expressed it. Suddenly we were too white for their liking, this vanguard often composed of white men and women themselves. The only thing worse was when they worshipped the ground we walked on. What's left is altogether benign and mundane, I'll be the first to admit, but since when did Borgloon and I care if something was *de rigueur* or not to be to our liking?

I respected Roddy's zeal but I had no patience for these causes that were becoming fashionable (they smacked of undiscerning clubism). To me, arriving at the right conclusion was for nought if you did not come about it legitimately, through pertinacious individualism. Everybody had to take a stand for some thing or other, God forbid you be ignorant on these matters. Didn't rub someone's nose in on their absorption in a tyrannized life, that sort of rot. The problem with cultural ascendency is that all the bozos start getting on the train. A lot of Roddy's associates were holding what I called "slummocking contests:" who could sink into squalor the fastest, who could ape the working class more convincingly, secure the job that sapped the most physical labour out of them. Studholme left a job in high finance to become a longshoreman! I had never seen anything like it (he used to crawl into bed next to me smelling to high heaven of fish) and I had to break his heart over it. My point is that although Borgloon was better than most pietists, this was a small consolation to someone like me. The least deluded person in the room still partakes in the grand delusion, after all. With any luck, I will have explained my frame of mind during this turbulent time with some degree of preciseness, if not detachment.

I put two years—not so long a time as one would think—between the pregnancy and seeing Roddy again, years when I desperately tried not to think about his rack and ruin whenever I was reminded of him. It was nearly impossible, but I forced him out like any other thing worth doing—sort of like a bad way you'd been doing fractions. I was huddled in the corner of a St. Clair dance club one evening, I guess it would be about 1977, 1978. I just remember that Bill C-150 was still in the news almost ten years later, so old wounds were starting to open again. I was cramped on one end of a counter that curved around a diamond-shaped bar. I saw that across from me Roddy was nursing a bottle of Zundert.

I was unfazed by the coincidence. After a few years living here, you become completely familiarized with the lengths to which the city will tinker with you—it's still too tiny even with its corners stretching far and wide like a choked balloon. I think it was my ability to focus a lapseless conviction that allowed me to talk to him. I wasn't planning on anything beyond a verbal confrontation. I pushed my way through the crowd to his side and without turning to look, I remember how in a practised, incurious way between sips, he greeted me with "What it is, what it is."

I steadied my hand on his wrist. "Look at me, Roddy."

He tittered behind the bottle at the mention of his name, which he brought across his face as one would defend themselves from a doust across the chin. "Roddy, listen to me. I came over because I know the least you could do is stand me some drinks."

He agreed before recognizing me, like this was a common occurrence with women approaching him in strange bars. He was chuckling while sifting through the receipts in his wallet. "You still drinking the same?"

When the drink came, I knocked it over with my elbow. This really tickled Roddy.

"I'll have another," I said.

Roddy took up the glove because I appealed to his competitive nature. I knocked over the next Nick and Nora glass too. Roddy continued to foot the bill, and was still not pressing the matter. I was within an ace of a slap in the face though, I can tell you that much. The barkeep made a motion with his hand to chastise me when he gathered up the shattered glass, but Roddy took him by the scruff of his neck and shoved him into the people sitting on the barstools next to us.

The third drink I actually tasted, and I could tell that Roddy was both prepared to finish this absurd game of hawk-dove as the winner, but also relieved that he would not waste an entire packet of wages on a matter of personal pride. This rigmarole continued for a few minutes more, but I had moved on to taking sips of my drink, and then emptying its contents into Roddy's beverages, spoiling them for him.

"That's enough, Cheree! When I get back, we're going to stop this foolishness. You looking for a handout for your kid, I don't blame you."

Roddy hot-headedly navigated the way to the toilet. When he was gone, I told a few people, the barkeep included, that I wanted to buy them all a round of their pleasure to make up for the disturbance. This was mostly received with nervous approval, barkeep's face in particular turning to sour mush. I sat there for a few moments, waited for when he ducked down to fetch some glasses, and then swiftly exited the Maple Leaf Ballroom, putting the entire episode—minus the priceless look on Roddy's soz- zled face I would have to imagine to see—behind me.

I really expected this to be the last of Roddy's hide or hair in my life. I am not a vindictive person by nature (turnabout is fair play). I dispelled the possibility of future engagements with my former lover-leman. If we were walking on the same street, why I would just cross over to the other side and look away. That's how big I was prepared to be about it. I knew he would never step through the club again, even if you crossed his palm with all the silver in the world. What had transpired between us hadn't been notable enough for me to rationalize avoiding going there, though. It was one of those insignificant episodes that dotted my life, not to say I was prone to such retributions.

I found myself at the Ballroom again for a work function a few months later. It was Lotte's bachelorette party, one of the other girls in my boss' typing pool. The recognition of knowing that we were in the exact same place where Roddy had received his comeuppance wasn't worth it, as I had come to enjoy myself. I barely got inside and ordered a drink when a man strode purposefully toward me and grabbed my arm so abruptly that he cracked a bone. He dragged me along with him like he was being pursued by dogs of war. I was about to cry foul when I caught the profile of his face and recognized him for the bartender Roddy had manhandled. I expected he was going to have choice words. I was prepared to take it in stride, but then was seized by a panicked notion that Roddy had caused a more sensational scene than I originally gave him credit for. We stopped in a dining alcove by a framed Konůpek print that helped steady my wandering eye as the barkeep began to twaddle away. I wasn't listening when he put money into a payphone, pulled out a card from his wallet and dialled a number. He handed me the receiver and blocked my way with his arm. I stared at his heaving chest as the dial tone gave way to a voice that spoke too closely to the mouthpiece.

An hour later I was picked up by 13 Division. They wanted to know anything I could tell them about Roddy. I was there to fill in the blanks, so I had them return the favour. Someone in the bar had seen Roddy plonking down cash hand over fist, first for my drinks, then for Mr. Nervig (the barkeep)—double shots of Seagram's—and five other patrons. Roddy seemed unperturbed by the expenditure. On his way out, he had been followed and felled a few blocks west of the bar near Oakwood Ave. He was knocked unconscious with a brick. The officers wanted to know what I could tell them and if I thought there was a pre-existing relationship with his attacker or with Nervig.

"Double neg-a-tive," I said.

I am not an unfeeling person, you have to understand; I would have been moved by far less cruelty. Through some first-rate sleuthing (the investigating officer told me), I was able to find the hospital Roddy was checked into, and was met with disapproval by the hospital staff. One nurse upbraided me with having taken so long to visit Roddy. It turned out I was Roddy's first visitor since the accident. Pathetic could not begin to describe the affair, even if most of Roddy's family, excepting his mother, weren't even on the continent. Roddy remained in a coma for several weeks after my visit, and awoke to permanent damage to his left eye, some clotting in the brain and neurological difficulties (the effects of which would not reveal themselves until more time passed). I was told I should be incredibly patient with Roddy and expect a long, unpredictable way ahead. They assumed I was his legal guardian and I didn't argue the point.

Fate intervening like this often chastens one's attitude, but this wasn't the case with me. I felt no compulsion to feel guilt over lightening the money in Roddy's pocket. I wasn't going to accept ownership of that. Religion hadn't been in my life long enough to knock that much sense out of me. All the same, I took Roddy into my home because as far as I could tell, he had nowhere else to go. He said he couldn't let his mother see him in this state. Nor did he have any of the same friends as when I knew him (shocking). They either tired of his grandstanding or were excommunicated as quislings from his inner circle. The housing arrangement was supposed to be for only a few days, or until he got back on his feet, whichever came sooner.

What happened when we went to his home address was that his landlady said she'd deposited all his things on the curb weeks ago and had leased the apartment to another tenant on account of Roddy being out of contact and not paying his rent. She assumed he had abandoned the unit. I told her the unvarnished truth and she said she regretted what had happened, but there was nothing she could do; in the eyes of the law, she was in the right. She advised that if we didn't want all our dirty immigration secrets coming out, we'd do well enough to stay away. I was unsurprised by the nature of the insinuation: I'd looked for apartments before. It was an easy thing to steal her welcoming mat and throw it into some bushes a block away. So while I wasn't overwrought with emotion about my hand in Roddy's injury, I was not prepared to have his imminent homelessness on my conscience just yet, even if I suspected a few nights living with me gave Roddy no end of satisfaction. This surely tipped the score back in his favour. Everything happened so quickly, I couldn't find the time to think of an excuse.

During this residency at my Pelham Park apartment, Roddy and I became close for the first time. We talked without reservation about our families (he could not stop asking questions about my father, the Derwish), our long-term plans (whether we would be staying or going back to Antananarivo/Pereybere), the sort of childhoods we'd had, and in turn, what sort of child we would have theoretically raised had things shook out differently. I found that we shared several things in common and this made having him in my house easier to bear (the nine months we spent together previously weren't spent talking). I helped Roddy with his disability applications, but they were all rejected saying he was able-bodied. I made sure we kept all his medical appointments in a logbook, and I prepared all his meals for him. The downside to this living arrangement was that it helped me understand the maximalist type of politics Roddy espoused.

Like a lot of immigrants, he had not been treated well. Lump of labour, slurs, beatings, he'd seen it all. He believed all the whites had an axe to grind against us, that there was something in their blood that made them want to bring the whole world to heel. It wasn't that I hadn't experienced the same thing, but I also knew that you couldn't throw people together like that, that you had to be very careful how you phrased certain things if you wanted to be taken seriously or not fall into the trap of the crimes of the accused. Anything that explained too much in the way of analysis probably wasn't worth the paper it was written on anyway. Roddy's handle on how racialization occurred was inconsistent and gestational, constantly resetting and coming-into-being. This made for poor listening. I preferred to let people put their feet in their mouths before I judged them too harshly. Then again, it wasn't as if I was prepared to let anyone wear the mark of Cain for an eternity. Just because one person was a prat didn't damn his whole tribe to foolishness.

I would say something I thought was fairly innocuous by way of counterpoint—say that where we came from didn't make what we had to say more valuable, what others had to say less so, at least not as a hard-and-fast rule, unless we wanted to get nowhere fast. This kind of provocation would make him erupt like a man possessed with the spirit of the devil himself. He would storm and rage and heap his accusations together in the crucible of his trauma-nudged brain and then send them half-formed into the world. "You know what you are, Cheree, you—you think you're a tall poppy and that if you have enough grit with your oats, you'll make something of yourself. And you might, but you'll always be the song, not the singer."

I only had to contradict him to be shut out completely. I came to believe his nominal values had nothing to do with the kind of person he was. His temperament was one that thrived on conflict and forced him to see what he was made of. I had never met someone so insecure about who they were, someone who needed such constant validation for his understanding of personhood while simultaneously inflicting violence to that conception.

> *On the subject of sleeping with white women:* "They're just looking for some slum gully to pick out their teeth later. Lord help me if we don't all go hungry once they develop a liking for the taste."

On the subject of white plenitude: "The whites have never had their status positioned as relational, fungible with lesser others. Potato famine, Holodomor, these are what I call minor oblations to God. Look how these so-called afflicted peoples come back to wreak vengeance on the coloured world. They can't even die like regular people."

On the subject of white liberalism: "I'm not here so you can take a hazard-free picture with me to shave a few points off your white-guilt card. Enlightenment isn't a fucking beauty pageant among yourselves. It's a cudgel I wield to bludgeon your face with!"

On the subject of white essentialism: "White consciousness is what I call a ravenous monism. If you are not careful, it will devour you and before you know it, you will be picking wild mushrooms and citing the Bavarian Purity Law at supper time."

The hostilities grew between us until I could no longer tolerate being called on the carpet in my own home. He wasn't just a bad guest, he was impeding my ability to have company (he would pick a fight with everyone that came over). I knew things could not stand as they were for much longer. Enduring the feeling that I was beneath his contempt because we did not observe the same political pieties was out of the question. I felt like I was reliving our relationship again.

Then one day a woman claiming to be Roddy's mother showed up at my door. Roddy left without so much as a belated "thank you" for putting him up and feeding him for three months. Strangely, I began to miss his presence. I had never had anyone waiting for me in the apartment after I returned from work and Roddy was the first man I ever laid with. I quickly overcame this outpouring of sentimentalism, though. I got on with my life and privately swore I would not see another Malagasy man again socially, cursing Roddy for colouring my mind with his attitudes, a thing I vowed would never happen.

The next time Roddy came crashing through my life—yes, he did come back—was a little under a year later. He was waiting on my stoop as I returned from buying groceries, and asked if I could put him up again for a few nights since his latest housing situation had fallen through. I was circumspect about letting him into my home again, so asked instead how his health was doing.

"I don't trust doctors to go nosing around where they shouldn't be, and then charge me medicine money for the pleasure. What a hup-ho world we live in."

He appealed to my growing insecurities and sense of worthlessness living in a city that seemed to compound my difficulties as a single woman advancing beyond her "prime" (that, and it seemed like he was in desperate need of a bath). I was starting to exhibit some of the world-weariness he had displayed a year before. Perhaps on account of this symmetry and my growing loneliness, I agreed to his staying on the condition he leave after a week.

I found Borgloon to be very withdrawn this time around, even totally expressionless. I began to ask myself if something drastic had occurred to him. This could have been made more prominent because of the contrast in his personality and behaviour. We did not discuss where he was living before, as I was mostly occupied with work (I left the typing pool and was now employed at a busy government office). This time he provided for himself in the way of food and drink. I threw out the newspapers in the house so that nothing could incite a dia-tribe, and made sure never to be inside when the nightly news came on. These precautions proved unnecessary, however— Roddy was a model guest. We did not discuss politics at all. I assumed he finally learned some manners and decided not to provoke his host needlessly. He helped with the washing up and was quiet when I retired to bed while he stayed awake drinking tisane, watching Al Waxman on *King of Kensington*, or *Front Page Challenge*.

On what was to be the agreed-upon final night of his stay, he warily came into my bedroom. He waited at the door and asked if he could come in.

"What's the matter?" I demanded.

He made no reply and sat at the foot of the bed. He began massaging my feet. I found the gesture disarming and pleasur-able at the same time. I was moved by how companionable he was being. We ended up almost going to bed together, but at the last minute something came over me, maybe a remembrance of our earlier indiscretion. I pushed his hands away gently and declined his advances. He stopped, then continued to caress my belly while he lay beside me. We fell asleep together in the bed for what seemed the briefest of moments, and then sexual con-tact resumed, though in an abbreviated, less stimulating fashion that made it impossible for a second offence. As he finished on my stomach, he mumbled into my ear, "You are my bitch of infinite resignation?"

The following morning, Roddy left the apartment to do God knows what. All that was missing from the apartment were a few loaves of bread and some cold cuts from the fridge. Between this and the final time Roddy came to visit me, I thought of him often and more fondly than I had been accustomed. I was scared that I was going to die alone and unloved in a country that passed me over for being unversed in its ways, undesirable in its conceptions of beauty. I had laboured contract after contract in different offices doing secretarial work, and it seemed as if I would never be on the same playing field as the whites. It's not that I began to wonder if there was a ring of truth to some of Roddy's ideas, it's that I was worried that if I didn't advance in society, I would turn into him and be eaten from the inside by the violent emotions that stirred.

But then I met Ousmane, who couldn't be more different from Roddy if he tried, and I realized what a mistake it would have been if Roddy and I had somehow stayed together. I was living with Ousmane for a little over a year, and we were expecting the birth of our first daughter, Nora, when we heard a knock on the door. No one was more surprised than I that Roddy had returned. I took the first time for a one-off situation primarily about getting even, and the second for an apathetic attempt at reconciliation. He looked ghastly. Undernourished and unkempt. I could smell him through the door. The most noticeable feature, though, were the gummas that deformed his face. I had never seen anything like it before. I didn't understand what they were, I just knew they were horrid and made looking at Roddy directly in the face a murderous task.

Ousmane had seen enough of these symptoms in Djibouti to take a pre-emptive position about the whole thing.

He stepped in front of me and ordered Roddy to leave at once. Roddy became agitated and emotional. Ousmane, not really knowing what to do, took the coat rack by the door and flung it in Roddy's direction. Roddy lurched forward with his torso, not really threateningly, but Ousmane put his whole back into getting Roddy to clear the entrance of our apartment. Then my husband slammed the door and fastened the lock. We looked through the peephole to see Roddy emerge from the cocoon of our coats he'd become entangled in. He screamed into the door for several minutes before leaving, taking the welcome mats from all the other units with him.

I asked if Ousmane was sure about what was wrong with Borgloon; he said of course that he wasn't, but that I should get checked if Borgloon was whom he suspected. "You can only use your cock as a divining rod for so long before it catches up with you."

I had never heard my husband speak so coarsely before. I tried to tell Ousmane that I was fine: the first prenatal visit would have alerted us to anything, and unless it could be transmitted by the shaking of hands, the last time I was with Roddy wouldn't amount to anything. Ousmane, who was known for a clinical disposition in all matters facing his private life, was ready to go around the bend, so I did what I was told and came back with the paper to prove it.

This incident with Ousmane was the very first time I ever felt shame in my dealings with Borgloon. I believed I had turned my back on someone who needed my help, which would have cost me almost nothing. The last thing he needed from someone he trusted was childish repugnance. I kept telling myself that Nora was my priority, and that I would have to do whatever it took to mentally and physically prepare to bring her into the world. This meant Borgloon falling by the wayside, constituting a distraction. And like with most things that did not immediately pertain to my advancement or happiness, I did not give much thought to Roderick "Borgloon" Rabinur in my later stages of life: nineteen years' worth of not caring in fact, an onerous legacy to stare in the face.

Other events outstripped the traces of Borgloon's impression, and I looked upon all the calamity and cause for celebration that I had wrought—a marriage, a divorce, widowhood, the death of my father, two fully grown children, one of diminished standing in our family because of choices I could not approve of, a blossoming and bloomed career in the civil service, a life-defining friendship with my friend Rhonda—with the admiration that comes with knowing there was not one thing that gathered about my life which wasn't of my own making. Despite these regrets, a part of me still feels as though I don't have to justify the tack I took with Borgloon. Nineteen years on and I still think his politics are shit. I don't disagree with them, but I feel the conclusions they led him to bear the distinct marks of laziness.

The Borgloon I remembered believed that to be whole, someone else had to be incomplete, and he had been living with a lack so large that you could hide fifty broken consciousnesses inside it. It was someone else's turn to chomp at the bit. Conformity was the mark of a weak intellect, assimilation was a subterfuge. Never back down. Never double back. Disappear beyond the even tenor of life, forward into an irrefragable tomorrow. These tenets align well enough with my own, but Borgloon used it as a pretext to treat people shoddily. I know that I had done the same thing to him through other motivations, but at least I knew I could be an asshole—Borgloon pretended he wasn't familiar with the term. I suspect that being on the right side of history doesn't count for much if you act like a tosser half the time. Borgloon's ideas, or better yet, those which influenced him and which he borrowed, gained traction over the years, and all these bloody contrarians fancying themselves Davids to society's Goliaths started coming out of the woodwork. This only further aggravated my feelings on the subject.

As I have said before, it's possible that on some level I resented Borgloon for his worldview more than for any one act he committed against me, that for the purpose of denying there being some inherent quality that governed us and conferred honorific this-ness and that-ness, I put up an impenetrable wall around myself. I never let anyone else define who I was or could be, even if it would serve my interests in the long run. That kind of political conniving will blot out the sun before it lays hands on me. So maybe I didn't reject a sick and afflicted Borgloon. I sent him to damnation because I didn't like the colours on his mast. This gives me a queasy feeling inside. It makes me feel petty and unresourceful. It tells me that I stood for nothing except apart from Borgloon—a negative philosophy whose adoption is not a particularly hard thing to do. I made nothing of myself in its stead, and in the dark of creation, I let a man who no one cared about sink into the rot and despair of destitution. Yet what I still mostly remember is what a heel he was. We're all only human, I suppose.

I don't know what roads Roderick ended up at exactly, what laid in store for him. He probably died like a dog in the streets, his head swollen and distorted beyond recognition. I do know that for a time he lived in a tent in Queen's Park with the johns and hustlers and cocksuckers for company. He had a companion in the end, a woman covered in chancres who was devoted enough to live outside in the Canadian winter with him begging for change, and whom he, for a reason no one has been able to determine yet, half-strangled to death one morning until she was able to fight him off and flee. She sought nearby shelter at the Women's College Hospital a few blocks from where they were camped out.

It took nineteen years for this tinkering coincidence to find me, for Sveta to call me on the phone one day making no sense whatsoever about how she had come into work and witnessed a frantic woman in tears screaming, "Borgloon trynna kill me!" at the top of her lungs. The blood drained right out of Sveta's face because that was not a name she had heard in almost a decade. She thought of me afterwards and found my number through Barbara, whom Ousmane had taken as his second wife after he had used her to desecrate the memory of his first, only to drop dead from a heart attack a few months later.

Sveta was as unreliable as they come, but she never lied about Borgloon when we were "all pointillists in the Borgloon picture," as she used to put it. Sex made her walk and talk the straight and narrow unlike most people. When she said that Borgloon made his way into the hospital after chasing his partner across Grosvenor Street looking like a ghoul advancing through a lazar house and wearing a T-shirt for a bandana that read *Apex Novelties*, I knew for sure it was him. I was working on the third floor of Whitney Block at this time—I had come a long way. It was no effort at all to come running down to meet Sveta and see him with my own eyes.

The security staff of the hospital were very patient with Borgloon, mainly keeping him at a safe distance from Shanna, the woman he came to retrieve and who stoutly believed he'd come to finish the job he'd started. Borgloon was just pacing around menacingly. Sveta was huddled in a corner while I was mesmerized by the flood of memories dancing in my head: his stapled jodhpurs, being alone at my first prenatal visit, knocking over his drinks at the Maple Leaf Ballroom, his convalescence at my apartment, stealing the Pelham Park welcoming mats. My reminiscences ended when I heard Borgloon muttering to himself something about there being no way Le Rallic is dead because "Shanna is French and she doesn't do the dishes." I unravelled when I heard this gibberish.

I almost traversed the invisible boundary separating the onlookers and guards from Borgloon, but my feet were fastened to the floor. He was practically a Swiss watch when I kicked him out of my apartment compared to the pig's breakfast of a man he'd become. All so suddenly it became incidental if Borgloon was right about the causes of his afflictions and trials. Perhaps it wasn't even important if my own ideas about how Borgloon got to where he got to were correct, what exactly led him there be it disease, injury or societal indifference. In the end, the fact that he was slogging the pathways of a park in the dead of winter living in a jerry-rigged tent was all that should have mattered.

With more deliberating than I care to admit, I decided that I would bring along a thermos of soup and some *poisson sale* in a container the next day for Borgloon. I packed these away in my purse with care, rode the subway to work and sat with apprehension thinking on the many ways the meeting could go. I left my home earlier than usual so that approaching Borgloon would not affect my work schedule. I gave it an hour. I disembarked, walked out of the station and crossed over to the Ontario legislative building and passed Wellesley. I went tromping through Queen's Park checking all the benches, above and behind trees, and beneath the monuments for a sign of Borgloon's existence. I found nothing.

I didn't have the strength to go combing through hospital registries on my lunch hour every day. I made a half-hearted call to Rhonda and asked if she had ever met someone matching Borgloon's description at St. Alban's, the homeless shelter where she worked. She said that if my life ever depended on giving a description of a stalker who was terrorizing me, they would have arrested him, made a movie about his life and sold his letters before they dug up my remains. Then she hung up the phone. I have not seen him again to this day, and I don't expect to tomorrow.

Sentiments and Directions from an Unappreciated Contrarian Writer's Widow

WIDOWSHIP

A life in harmony with others is a wasted one.

One husband's sanctimony is another's daily bread.

A man's character is usually the opposite of that which masquerades on his face; for this reason, moderation appears to be the greatest of hidden human faults, while it is at the same time the most difficult to apprehend.

Learn to depend on disappointment, if only to disappoint others.

Apparently, never let an opportunity go by to befoul a well-heeled fellow's banquet table.

A grudge can give one's life purpose and, most invigorating of all, the conviction to believe in their own hypocrisy.

A poor liar has the entertainment of others as his sole comfort.

The worst thing about growing older is expecting that the world is beholden to you for growing more intractable and even-minded about your faults.

A man free of complaint is like a hog without a trough.

Death is the reward to those who constantly expect the best possible outcome in all enterprise.

The greatest gift a father has ever given his son is a willingness and model against which to stray.

HOW FARES THE COMPANION?

We pine for the deleterious failures of our closest companions so that they will both understand our suffering and pay homage to our resolve.

To repay a friend's confidence with secrecy is worse than betraying their trust.

Be wary of anyone bearing gifts, be irreconcilable to anyone bearing advice.

PASSIONS IN DECLINE

The passions are like carcasses resurrected by forgetfulness, not unlike one's progenitors.

The passions can unseat only the mind that expects anything less from that great motive power and does nothing to indemnify itself against their will.

Intemperance is an affliction of the soul that bestows even the most inane and vapid of activities with the sheen of an unobserved novelty.

Avarice seldom exists unaccompanied by a rearing vainglory.

An egotist is not so appalling a creature because he is never responsible for his failures, but because such accidents to his person further his bewitchment.

A man free of obligations is not a liberated one: he is simply a bastard.

One should manage their desires as they would honour the dying wish of a mortal enemy.

Love is Pride's way of acknowledging excellence in connoisseurship.

There may not be much glory in a bottle, but enough to make glory seem like a fool's errand.

There is no worse abjection or greater triumph than feeling unloved.

There is no more powerful inclination to stolidity than compassion and thoughtfulness in all endeavours.

SOCIETY PARLANCE

Silence is not an invitation to speak nor a substitute for eloquence.

Boisterous people are to be avoided as if stupidity was catching.

Ignorance is like an untapped reserve that can encompass any depth of delusion.

There is no greater impertinence than to be kept waiting.

No one is more eager to believe their own twaddle than someone who appears to gain the least from it.

Romanticism is the solution to all of life's problems if one is inclined to evade them entirely. In other words, it is just another way to beautify scoundrels.

It is better to be an afterthought to your enemies than to be treated as if you were a curiosity.

Ingratitude is the way to pay a compliment while living among barbarians, gratitude the means to exact revenge while living with the civilized.

Obligations were created for no better purpose than to clarify our disdain for one another.

Good taste accentuates everything currently outside of one's possession, bad taste everything within grasp.

There are always people who are impeccably indisposed to do anything of value in life except fret about people indisposed to do anything of value in life.

A modest favour cannot take the air of a tradition any more than it can a king's pardon.

Sententiousness comes at the price of poor conversation.

A millennium of philosophical thought has still not found a remedy to the pretence of babbling coherently.

Exhortations shape history much in the way that thieves declaim stolen goods.

The indignities of living are so abundant that surprise in any situation is a fair appraisal of an individual's artlessness.

There are as many dullards in the world as there are gaps in one's thinking.

The world is a misbegotten accident, but no more so than is desired.

Never call unannounced unless you are repaying the favour.

An affectation gives purpose to the purposeless and so too to his accuser.

We treat our errors as if they were accidents but view our accomplishments as if they were the product of meticulous planning, when it is the exact reverse that holds true.

One's mettle usually counts for far less than the ability to dispatch this resolve in an apposite setting.

TREASURES OF LEISURE

Even a fruitless task can edify the mysteries of indolence.

One must shake the scholarly pursuits as one would an infection or a companion who has outlived his use.

The impulse to collect artifacts and memories about us is a desire to erect a monument to our own recklessness; not so that we may silence this lurid activity, but so that we may lay our heads on its altar.

Expectation and hope are generally very stupid uses of one's time.

Reminiscence is death a thousand times over.

Many a tried path has led to disaster, but only the untrodden road can render one's misfortune truly exquisite.

MASOCHISM, MEANING AND PURITY

It is the privilege of the damned to be able to alleviate the
misfortunes of their countrymen and enlarge them upon
their enemies. A competent writer on the other hand can find
significance in every which thing. Taken together, such an
individual should be indomitable.

Experiencing literature is a very sobering experience: it
answers questions life has articulated with the clarity and
fitfulness of a stumbling drunk, and reiterates those questions
with the clarity and fitfulness of a rambling one.

There are some writers who take to the pen to settle scores,
others to elaborate on their own conditions and still more who
seek to communicate their intentions for the sallies of fame.
None, however, are more effective than those who feel this
compulsion as supremely as the pangs of masochism.

It is an ill sign for a writer to have no one to call on for advice,
company or repudiation.

If one regards failure as an antecedent to success, they have
never known either.

The wise are never so clever as when they belie iteration for
mastery.

There are as many uses for a pen as a gallbladder.

A diffuse and meandering preamble is the noetic equivalent of whistling in the dark.

There are times when the literary arts hum the plangent tones of misery like a cracked drum over the distant roll of thunder.

The myth of inspiration's wayward muse is the closest cure to dilettantism as we are likely to produce, so we would do well to perpetuate it.

A life spent composing aphorisms is a happily wasted one.

Imagination is formlessness in a void of self-absorption.

All meaning is created through crisis and diffusion.

All purity is created through resemblance and disavowal.

There are no new ideas, only unusual ways of forgetting.

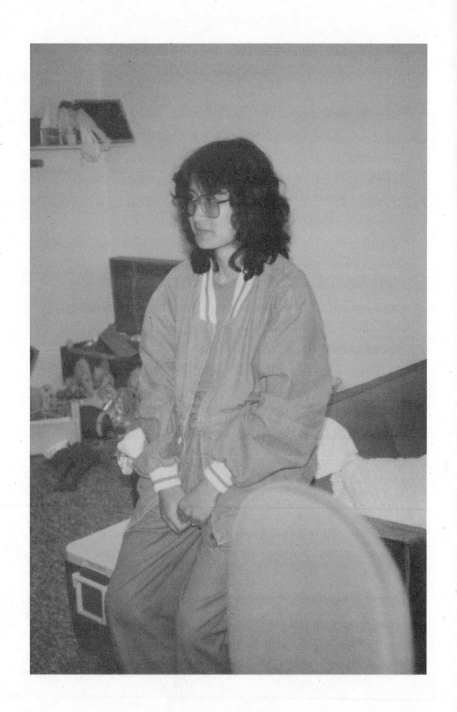

A Defence of Misanthropy

PUGILISM

On the subject of my misanthropy, I have formed attentive if imperfect ideas, which according more to the spirit of its remedial qualities than to any other feature, I have incorporated to a progressive degree in my disposition to others, my outlook toward the world and my assessment of my own mental fitness. As a concept of some ill repute—a refuge for those who cannot satisfy the many demands impressed on them by modern living—a defence in the most popular sense of the word would imply its claims required definite qualification, or a justification of behaviour that when the mind is under the duress of punitive action, can serve to release the balance of a bad debt. But as there are no obligations in whose custody I must presently satisfy, the form of this "defence" is neither vindicatory nor in the nature of clarification; historically descriptive at times, perhaps—what has been written before on the subject not having been lacking in enumerating the social tendencies of the misanthrope—yet of what a misanthrope might "owe" to those who speculate on her actions is of no real concern, for who so dares possess the pathetic patience for imagined slights damns themselves to, it hardly needs mentioning, an ignoble failure.

The defence of which I speak, and wherein I am in earnest to make, pertains to how misanthropy has availed me against the

many noxious influences the world has on offer, namely petti-
ness, baseness of character, short-sightedness, improvidence,
cupidity, graft, pusillanimity, ingratitude, physical violence,
prurience and treachery; how such an attitude, the fondness for
the collective views which comprise it, has prevented me from
living too inclement a life insofar as an outlook is able to fare—a
defence in the *pugilistic* sense of the word.[1]

PRAXEOLOGY

The account I mean to give is descriptive of my worldview; it is
entirely praxeological in nature and contains within it no word
of solicitation or appeal to a higher ethics, despite how vocif-
erously I champion its favour (I anticipate this finickiness will
not be met happily). Perhaps it is enough to say that one cannot append to moral dictums a seal of immoderate approval any
more than one can trace its authority to unshakeable grounds
(i.e. a taboo or worse, a *virtue*), other than the source in which
its textual origins reside. This is certainly not what constitutes
a compelling description of a subject's properties, *viz.* a natural kind. Hence, the question, "What is the good life?" may be

---

1   These remarks may be conceived as a vindication by any other name;
    when someone affirms that they are a misanthrope, their words are
    immediately taken to be exculpatory: "She cannot despise people to
    an apogean degree"—a familiar bromide. "How can you be a misan-
    thrope and not cloister yourself from the world?" "You are admitting
    defeat by refusing to stand against the injustice that daily attends our
    sorrows," and more of the same vapidity, whether I have invited such
    an inquisition or not.

reformulated as the consequentialistic, "What and to whom is the good life *good for*?"

More often than not considered a philosophical dead end, misanthropy on an intuitive level is not so appalling an idea when it is encountered that mankind is hardly expected to form close attachments to everything with which it comes into contact. The variety we must confront daily provokes numberless responses that cannot without grim difficulty be resolved into an encompassing approbation for all things. Neither have misanthropy's pollutant consequences germinated into great holocausts or massacres for that matter (differentiating here between a hatred of humanity *qua* humanity and hatred of particular groups contained within it). Similar to the reflexive action of all ideas originating in forbearance, it is enough to say that such a model of action operates within the confines of the degrees of success and failure befitting the individual's will power, to say nothing of the moral value (if any) representative of the act itself. Misanthropic actions originating in restraint and forbearance should classify as supra-moral acts over and above the ambit of regulated ethical behaviour (unlike say non-interventionism or conscientious objection, which locate its motivations entirely within an ethical framework).

To the extent a misanthrope relieves the world of the burden she embodies—in the sundry ways that beings are burdensome by merely expending numinous and material resources— misanthropy requires no more an account of the actions it stimulates than the effects of the sun on our native soil do. One does not arraign the sun on regulatory offences of sunburns or phosphenes, but merely accepts its effects as part and parcel of its daily operations. It is the degree to which an individual is exposed to its rays that determines the resulting harm, and the misanthrope should relinquish all responsibility for the effects of those who hazard prolonged contact with her blistering irascibility.

BULWERS AND ALGERS OF THE WORLD

When a misanthrope achieves her goal, still yet to be defined, it is for the most part achieved negatively and at her own expense. Misanthropy is but one of a thousand meagre enterprises raising hob with the influences at play on the planet, moved as we all are by the first of the Four Noble Truths; it is not the answer to all troubles, but rather another ingredient in the confluence of activity that shapes and rends the world alike—therewith one should not overstate its relative importance. If we can conclude that misanthropy is merely a productive measure by which to understand the difficulties in life and best surmount them, this shall constitute a victory for our purposes.

Though not as companionable an intellectual preoccupation as it once enjoyed in the eighteenth and nineteenth centuries— generally regarded to have been stamped out by a Victorian sensibility that found influences against the common weal unsupportable—it still remains unclear whether the Bulwers and Algers of the world would be afforded the same indulgence in a modern setting for their anti-misanthropic screeds. It seems rather more likely that they would be constrained to a sphere of dubious pettifoggery; yet if there was ever a time whose expostulations of hate could beget a legion of misanthropes, surely it would be that of our own?

And what is more, the world has been in no short supply of works occupied with fractured fraternities of man; one often wonders why this inclination is met with such costive hostility. Can there be a more availing protreptic against the vacillations, the tentativeness of human policies, than in the adventures of Candide in his search for his beloved Cunégonde? Or a more succinct development of these ideas than Mr. Hazlitt's famous deathblow to hope in the observation that customs will forever prevail over excellence (perhaps the greatest of secret sins that society has ever turned to mawkish account)? Why is it that the *anomie* of an opposing wind produces such disparate reactions in our fellows' breasts?

These misanthropic arguments—especially when rendered in appropriate literary style—are impregnable of doubt and suspicion; whose sun-kissed reasoning is often coruscating, but not to the extent that we may not follow its example. Misanthropy asks if it is not the case that humanity's lot turns on the aspiration to reposition one's relationship to others from that of being under the boot heel to that of delivering the pressure (if not in this active form of meting violence, then in abstaining to whatever degree possible), and if there is not something beyond this rudimentary arrangement. There is likely no more insulting an accusation than to be charged with a kind of guileless crudity in one's worldview if I am not very much mistaken.

MISANTHROPIC UNAVAILABILITY, DREAD AND EXILE

My misapprehension on the subject in part stems from fear of the charge that for all the time I have spent wallowing on this blighted orb, I have not grasped the organization of things well enough to understand how power and wealth are apportioned, how such guarantors of satisfaction work to better and worsen our lives, and always in stark, overbalanced arrangements. But fear is not enough of an incitement to action, incisive though its spurs may be. Fear of being insensate, or of being incorrect in one's conclusions, cannot carry one to the terminus of applied reason unless one's life is fulsomely dominated by dread. It is no great feat to witness the malice and perdition that exhaust the spirits of man and to evolve this view into a trenchant cynicism that can summon no witness to hope; it is but a short step to further amplify such views into a *bellum omnium contra omnes.*

Indeed, this is one kind of "unavailable" misanthropic response, tempting though it may be, represented abstractly by Molière's Alceste when he claims he must leave his home rather than endure the false witness of his peers. Exile cannot be deliverance for someone who mistrusts their fellows because her hatred of people who share common failings soon gives way to an abhorrence of herself and of her failure to stomach the polemical barbs of community. The central problem for a misanthrope seems to be how to reconcile her intolerance towards the majority of the world with its intolerance of herself.

SENECAN COMPROMISE

To put it another way, the Senecan solution to the predicament of whether one must "imitate or hate the world" is both: his sensible but in a way desperate counsel is to retreat inward where possible, but meet with others likely to improve yourself. There is an element of desperation to any compromise, in mitigating one's humours because it proves untimely or unfashionable; ultimately, in the realization that those who improve our constitution may prove insufferable people (Seneca's proposition is a convenient way out of the indictment though, that arrogance above mankind, not the hatred of it, is the misanthrope's true calling in life). This notion that misanthropy and sociability are not two worlds apart is based on the degree that it is presumptuous to state that society, in all its infinite evils, is so damning an influence as to lead one to extinguish all living claim to it. Beyond the fact that it is not clear how one would go about achieving a state of decivilization, what concept of social or personal utility would be rendered by fleeing from the obligations heaped on our backs remains unaddressed.

It is true, however, that Seneca's position removes a great many impediments that would otherwise hinder a convincing espousal of misanthropy. The goal of the misanthrope cannot be total abstraction but integration on some level: we must find a place within civilization that does not compromise our understanding, and the only way this can happen is for that relationship to persist. Meaning is best produced in general society, not in the void, and the only way to preserve one's hate is to renew overflowing justifications for hatred.

Modern individuals are expected to exercise the *agape* of a saint, forgiving all manner of calumniation, but surely the indulgence solicited on behalf of one person can be required of the other? To those who feel compelled to ask what justifies my alienation from their lifestyles, and what superciliousness governs my mind in passing judgement on them, one should recall that to suffer my thoughts (and to suffer them with civility and prepossession) is the greatest gift of any friendship, and on that account, can be expected in equal measure even if this hinges precipitously on the temper of minds that grace us for friendship's sake, and whether a misanthrope to the manner born can palliate her animosity.

STOCKDALE AND THE UNDEMEANED EXISTENCE

There is another historical positioning of the misanthrope that warrants analysis, and that is the question of whether they are comparable to the historical figure of the sage. It is worth remarking that there are indeed curious symmetries between the outlooks of these erudite hermits who would seek influence among learned corners of the globe, and those who would gladly have nothing to do with them. Misanthropy's philosophical roots are undoubtedly in self-examination and chastisement, *viz.* an impeccably Christian temperament. It is no wonder that a figure like Percival Stockdale took monumental strides to root misanthropic sensations in a kind of bifurcated dualism: a "seductive," obloquious kind of misanthropy in one corner, and a divinely commissioned one, heaven-sent with the sole purpose to beatify, on the other.

Stockdale is not wrong to make such a division, though the theological imputations of motive force, unsurprising in one whose vocational confidences exposed him to all manner of iniquitous behaviour, are poorly placed (his views shake out to little more than actions not contributing to the glory of God are unworthy of virtuous imitation). Worse than this transgression is the fact that the execution of his reasoning at times amounts to a kind of poor man's gnomic verse (his propensity for false consolation is astonishing). And yet, despite his failures as a proselytizer, who chose for a target perhaps the most difficult convert of all besides the infidel (such was the quality of its attractiveness), he commands respect for defending the tarnished cause of misanthropy with unyielding enthusiasm and arriving at conclusions that for the most part proved influential (he believed that misanthropy entailed a declaration of will that encouraged strident, necessary responses from its detractors—cheap political exhibitionisms aside—that would eventually lead to productive conversions).

It would also be neglectful not to acknowledge the fact that Stockdale's writings emerged from the exalted plane of the First Estate. The dismal prospects advancing behind the standard of the misanthrope could arguably stem from a kind of privileged boredom: a class character affording the ability to make certain "acquisitions" and then to tire of them as we tire of things: of conversations, of arguments, of people. Misanthropy does exist on the shoulders of wanting to be able to remove one's tethers in favour of a purer, undemeaned kind of existence, but class plays a role in the development of hatred only insofar as having means to channel this animosity and in what desired ways, not in what we choose as objects of scorn. One man's hatred of imbalance is another man's *raison de vivre*—just as one can prove hostile to niggardly social spending while another the entire concept of social insurance wholesale—because nature affords no limitations in the way of variety. It is always man's temper to hate, feel inadequate and act out jealously; class merely manifests how the means to revenge ourselves of inequity is directed. The misanthropic inclination, if I have argued my point correctly, is in fact cheerily non-denominational.

ARTICLES OF REASON

Now one must succumb to calls heard from both sides of the traverse. My misanthropy has not been advanced so far with any concrete means of the designs I have employed, something curiously absent from most buckram treatises on the subject. Indeed, there is a kind of waggish humour to avowals like, "avoid crowds" or "never engage in conversations in which more than two individuals are present." I suspect any enumeration of ideal misanthropic action would here begin to take on a farcical quality, but true enough, *generatim discite cultus.*

UNREGULATED LOATHING

Whereas others find tranquillity in meditation, vigorous physical exercise, postprandial conversation and wherever else they chose to find it, I have made my bed in an unregulated domain of loathing. To witness the unadorned meanness of spirit that pervades this century is harmful to one's constitution, this much is certain (I marvel at how great a store I possess of these same unfortunate qualities). When I prove more domineering than I knowingly wish to be, I understand this to be the true shade and dimension of humanity: all individuals of influence are notoriously unfledged. When ideals are like diversions and principles are but instruments lain dormant for future and fair usage, one can count on a broken destiny of weakness and contingency, where ignorance is borne with honour, misery heralded by triumph, shamelessness captive to no thrall. This produces nothing if not an anti-natalistic calm, and the desire to navigate only the most austere fairways of life.

INTRANSIGENCE AND GRIEVANCE

I have found it to be a good practice to hold on to grudges—for dear life if possible—despite thirty centuries of philosophical wisdom to the contrary. A grudge is a good way of reminding oneself that mankind never has your interests at the heart of its operations and will serve its priorities first, second and third before ever giving you a jot of consideration. A memory of someone ill-using you is integral in predicting patterns of comportment that tend to subsist among new and old contacts so that before the gavel is even raised, you can know the judgement before you. What better reserve is there than correct anticipation when no foolproof science of the mind is possible?

There are times when this foreknowledge will deceive you and lead you astray; times when you are willing to peer further into a relationship only to be rebuked; and still others when you back and fill between how best to employ your suspicions; but overall, the perfected mind is one that expects very little from others, apart from an intransigent unwillingness to change. One is proven wrong so infrequently on this count that the instincts can become a tasseography of (and a passport to) the future.

Not everyone can cast away relations that at one time rejoiced the heart or provided succour to trouble's heavy sorrows. I would myself not be able to shun others as easily as I do had I not received the same injuries first. We are constantly abused for our time at every turn, never given an allowance of thought. An abuse of time obliges you with returning the favour in kind, and in the end, some frustrated connections are better left that way.

ECONOMIES OF RESTRAINT

In the furore of empty deeds, there are some occupations doomed to the status of dire extravagance more than others; that is to say, they are the most bootless of human enterprises. Having absorbed myself in the *unappreciated* and *contrarian* enterprise of writing, I have become intimately acquainted with this reality. Would it not be more discreet to spurn the court of friends for a time when despair does not reign uninhibited? A calculating writer is predisposed to economies of restraint, so she closes her doors when her rancour is stirred to enmity-absorbing levels.

Living in the metropolis where there are no shortages of agreeable recreations, it becomes iconoclastic to spurn invitations: someone is always dying or being born, one's neighbours become associates, one's associates become intimate friends and one's intimate friends become entwined souls. For sanity's sake, a repulse can become a salvation, even if it makes us unneighbourly. A party, if properly managed, can be a splendorous engagement, though it depends on good, sound judgement to preserve you from harm, injury or worse: disconsolate boredom.

There are times in someone's company when the feeling of having exasperated the sentiments becomes palpable, and the need to break away becomes uncontrollable. Never spending more than a few hours in direct contact with someone whose faults bring the worst out in you can optimize and strengthen that relationship, giving it the tincture of unfamiliarity that will serve future encounters fittingly. There are some comrades who are desperately out of reach, whose company one yearns for, hoping to renew the bonds of intimacy; their companionship eludes us and we wax submissive to their vagaries, enslaved like a bureaucratic animal. On such occasions, misanthropy serves us in a surprising fashion: when we are reminded of these disappearances, we may fear that our misanthropy and disinclination to repair these connections will make us obdurate; we bridle at the thought of this hardness, and wish not to turn an idea that has served us so well into a millstone. These tiers of our thinking, moving away from how misanthropy can best serve us, to how its unchecked licence can prove antithetical to our goals, is necessary for any model that governs our desires and needs.

PHILONEISM

If one has the means, a situation in a quiet city can be an unexpected boon; this effect can only be amplified by devoting what time is at hand to reading, writing and light company. One can enlarge the mystic-minded pleasures of nature, the talents of intellection and the sensual philoneism of the world for a price that dwindles to nothing, inclinations to indolence notwithstanding. In truth, one is practically forced to misanthropy by virtue of living in any city where the cold dissolve of a hand-shake and other discourtesies keep people at arm's length. There is an implacable distance among men and women that seems to expand to the exact degree that a populace increases, for the tension of competing limited interests is not only multiplied, but so too is the strain of forming connections that move beyond the surface-skimming variety. The congeniality of an underclassed burg can undercut this roving loneliness dramatically with relationships that are in turn more fulfilling.

DEBILITY, TRADUCEMENT AND THE STEP
OF PROGRESS

It may also be worth mentioning that I have had the intoxicating benefit of several maladies, ranging from the rare to the common, befalling an already delicate constitution, which has only furthered the avoidance of my compeers; and when I was cured of an idiopathic paralysis or a hearing disorder, I still managed to eke out more time for companionless leisure. People shun others plagued with illness and give no second thought that this might be exactly the kind of attention they desire.

The greatest word in a misanthrope's vocabulary is undoubtedly "no." Judicious usage of it will preserve her quietude. A firm hand steadies an unbalanced heart, and she need only rate the laws of complaisance against what her susceptibilities will allow to reach a state approaching misanthropic grace. Regarding concerns of appearing uncivil, one must only consider that an individual who has been moved through the passions to kill is not so disconcerting as a hardened killer who stays his hand,

and likewise with the articulations of a misanthrope's *weltsch-merz*. Soon enough the refusals become a commonplace, and no longer carry the hyaline sting of ingratitude.

There is a kind of drabness behind the myth of sociality which states that company in another intellect's opacity is infinitely preferable to the familiarity of one's own thoughts; there is nothing that further gives lie to this proposition than the interminable discourses that run the gamut of repetitious articles to the poison of contrary minds. There is a very fine degree between when the lustre of elaborating a contrary stance on a subject proves inviting and when it does not. The majority of people do not want to suffer the obverse of their own striking personalities, and not just for the obvious reason of embellishing their egos, but because those associations prove in one form or another such an unflattering traducement against us. In the raging battle to convert the other to one's resident opinion, both realize the ineptness of their dispute, or how willing they are to sacrifice everything, friendship included, for the sake of surviving with their beliefs intact, such is our affinity for them. What is sometimes worse, those relations who form such a close alliance with our own sympathies can be rendered revolting when they do happen to diverge from our thoughts, however insignificantly. Mankind gravitates toward anything that can extinguish a darkening lack, but any recourse that temporarily succeeds in this effort only proves to us how formidable that absence is and will likely remain.

There is something unseemly about gregarious people who appear unable to be alone with their thoughts and who balk at the maturation of their minds. Platitudes abound of mankind being nothing if not social creatures, but that conceit seems to be little more than an overblown insurance policy against an empty home; in truth, man shares more common traits with a peacock than he does with any other creature, his social contract amounting to little more than a licence to maim and brutalize in a mannerly fashion. Large gatherings wreak havoc on the comely art of conversation, and dilate expressions of flattery to the exact extent that it retracts articles of good sense. There are so many interests reticulating that one must step around anyone else's prized stake; people do not speak plainly, but serve opening course after opening course of affected modesty before they can answer a question they forget was forged in the fires of their own arrogance to begin with.

The bustle of a crowd is like a thousand chiming bells drowning out every expression of thoughtfulness. People champion association as if it were the greatest human invention since the aqueduct, and although it is true that one necessarily flows from the other, as is the case with every itinerant step of progress, there is much to be said about the general result of coalitions, which is to have your resources absorbed into a vacuum. It is a good rule which states that most lives never bloom into harmony, and it is perhaps an even steadier maxim that one never really tires of their own company. The conclusion, if one is disposed to reach it, is not overly difficult.

SUPERFLUITY IS A STATE OF MIND

All these hurried brushes with the misanthropic persuasion occasion one thought above all: if this is integration, then a pincushion is likely to prove an apt metaphor for the misanthrope's state of mind. A misanthrope's spleen waxes and wanes like her other humours, and she alternately feels compelled to feel the sun's rays on her fingertips, the honeyed tones of her companions' musings or even to smear the mud of Camarina that is the awkwardness of human interplay over herself. The important thing is that such a return to society does in fact occur to serve as a reminder of who she is, and not, contrary to Seneca's admonition, always with minds that stand a likely chance to improve her own.

She is animated by a principle that makes her wary and tentative, soured by both experience and memory, yet she is perhaps more human than those who have yet to be disabused of the many illusions that sap the planet with straits of confusion. She is not in a slavish manacle to one idea of her choosing, unable to engage other opinions or understand them cogently; rather, she is a consolidated individual with eyes to see, ears to hear and a mind that is perspicacious to the truths that reveal themselves.

Howsoever a misanthrope appears symptomatic of a trend of receding civility, it is in fact far more accurate to describe her as a kind of woebegone pragmatist that feels entitled to speak plainly, if with a talent—a favour even—for brinkmanship. She shares in this respect the same claim to impertinence that both the simpleton and the iconoclast revel in, though to what degree she resembles one over the other we leave to the scope of her faculty and the tenor of her achievements. As a provident mentality, misanthropy is deficient in some respects, contrary to the natural gifts of communality; however, escaping the weaknesses of one's temperament is not always possible. Misanthropy is not an ennobled state that rouses an individual's movements, but more so a realization that it is better to be charged with condescension than charmless optimism under the conditions in which the world presently exists. Indeed, there are so few out-works against the incapacitating obstacles of the mind that one cannot begrudge an individual for finding sanctuary in an atti-tude that does not for once elaborate upon the human tendency to superfluity.

Mahebourg

CHANTEY

Banne instructions	Instructions
Pena l'importance	Don't matter
La vie pu fini tout to l'energie	Life will see to vigour
Romance ene	Romance is wont to
Grand la guelle	Blather about
De toute facon...	Anyway...

Mo vine ici	I came here
Pu le plaisir	For the pleasure
Mone finne critique	I got stick
Pu banne desordre	For the mess
Mo pas fine ajoute li	I didn't count
Dans mo compte	The ledger
Page sombre	The dark page
Pu tourner dans mo la vie	Will turn itself again

Garde bateau salete	Jailers of the junkboat
Marque l'entree	Mark the entrance
Avec ene la corde	With a rope
Raccroche telephone	Lay down the receiver
To fine prend mo la voix	My voice is now your own
Allez mo bane descendants	Go forth my descendants

Dans l'obscurite	Into the darkness
Et quand soleil fine coucher	And the gloom
Dialogues dans asoir	Dialogues in the dusk
Excitant l'esprit!	Excite the mind!
Instructions compte toujours	Instructions still matter
Sexe, carillons et ces balivernes	Sex, chimes and jive charisma
Désirs de toutes limites	Urges of every borderline
To pe badiner…?	You don't say…?
Mo fine vine ici	I came here
Pu so bon le temps	For the weather
Mo fine plein are stress	I got sick of the stress
Mo pas fine ajoute li	I didn't count
Dans mo compte	The ledger
Page sombre	The dark page
Pu tourner dans mo la vie	Will turn itself again
Garde bateau salete	Jailers of the junkboat
Marque bannes sorties	Mark the exits
Avec ene la corde	With a rope
Mahebourg pardonne	Mahebourg is forgiving
Pour bannes vivants	To the living
Et bannes damnes	And the damned
Eski to capave	Can you be
Separe la mer	The parting in the sea
Si tous dimounes	If everyone's
Ena connection avec sa crime la?	Connected to the crime?

All Songs by Kaartikeya Derwish (Mauritian Countryside Plenitude Publishing Company)

Ah-Sen and I

SCHOLARLY STYLE OF RECITATION

The one they call Ah-Sen is aggrieved by everything I do. My movements are marked by languor, unless ratified by our countless driven obsessions. For this, I am both feted and objurgated by the silence of a breath. I detest flattering gatekeepers for drops of their borrowed time, or puffing my chest out to castigators masquerading as writers; he endures these abasements, and at times, with rather good humour. I am better occupied in the company of my children, the films of Berlanga, the prose of Sitwell and Cendrars (Stevenson trailing not far behind). Ah-Sen validates these habits, but presides over them with the oppugnancy of a judge. I read for pleasure, while he labours under the *scriptible* sun of a bastard formalism, having been born under a mad sign. He would go years without finishing books, drowning at the level of the sentence, until I liberated him from the prison of his foolishness. I provide him with workaday sustenance, and keep vigilant watch over neglected pocketbook, and still find a never-ending reckoning of drink and debt threatening to make a mockery of my resolve. He is regularly absent when a question of manual labour arises. There will come a time of obeisance to his custom of warping the world and populating it with our enemies' drolleries. Voltaire wrote well when he said that if attacked on a matter of style, it is for the work alone to make its rejoinder. A style eternally grapples with the impossibility of its existence, the necessity of its destruction; it is an exercise in the parametrics of purity, the dialectics of forgetfulness. It is a belonging of oblivion and a flight of life. My grandfather incarnated Ah-Sen in 1949 to sustain himself in Africa. I incarnated him to sustain my appetite for vulgarism. I have no reason to unbridle myself from this tautological character who marshals my existence into something that is as "twisty and as hard to unravel as a Gordian knot."

I do not care which of us has written this page.

Sous Spectacle Cinema Research Consultation with Bart Testa

ON THE VIABILITY OF AN EXPLORATORY BUSINESS EXPENDITURE IN THE ARTS

The one thing I'd say about my publications, oddly enough, is they're not directly related to my teaching. I edited a book on Pasolini for example, though I've never taught Pasolini. The rank I hold is senior lecturer, an evolved position. I began as a tutor, then a senior tutor, then a senior lecturer. In a way, these positions were being invented while I was doing basically the same job. These titles all represent "the teaching stream," which is differentiated from the "professorial stream" or "tenured stream." I've not really been formally evaluated for my research and publications. That's just as well with me because I put almost all my academic energy into teaching, though I've written a fair bit.

I have done a wide range of teaching in film, and for about fifteen years I taught semiotics at Victoria College. Cinema Studies in the 1970s could be charitably described as an emergent field. It didn't develop the bells and whistles of a fully armed academic institution until the end of the seventies. It was understandable people would have a home discipline where they took their training and then focused on this novel area or added it on to their specialization. And that's pretty much how we got Cinema Studies going. The prominence of tutors in emergent fields of study, alongside professors who were experimenting outside their home discipline, was a result of this way of testing those fields, and college programs were a vital venue for all that.

Our program and its faculty are somewhat divided. Some of the people are inclined to formal and textual analysis and others are interested in the cultural resonances of films. Most of us examine both, but it is a matter of emphasis. In the most broad, generic way, people are interested in thematics, and people are interested in stylistics. I've always been a formalist. And that's, I think, really suitable for the place where I did most of my teaching—in the first- and second-year courses, teaching the rudiments of film analysis. I want to point out that this is the formal approach in literature by and large. I would assume that students in literature would be well grounded in the formal analysis of poetry, for example.

Cinema Studies, to a large degree, was initially generated out of New Criticism, and its parallels in the study of visual art. My principal influence as a graduate student was P. Adams Sitney, as well as figures like Annette Michelson and William Rothman, a student of philosopher Stanley Cavell. The key figures in the history of film theory—Münsterberg, Arnheim, Eisenstein, Pudovkin, Bazin, Metz, Mitry—theorize cinema on the basis of an idea, its character, and they get at that character largely through formal analysis. So for both reasons of the culture out of which North American film studies came—initially a literary studies culture—and because of the way in which cinema has been theorized from the 1920s until the 1970s, it has been rooted in formal method.

Therefore, Cinema Studies has a multifaceted inheritance from formal analysis and that's woven into how it exists as serious intellectual discourse. It's how it announced to the world that it was worthy as an academic discipline in terms of its core methodology. My idea of purgatory would be to sit around with students who had just graduated from high school to get their interpretations of the movies. I can't think of a bigger waste of time for me or for the students. Instead we work through formal questions. Why? Because their idea of interpretation has been an unholy alliance between what they *should* think about things in the world, and the treatment of works of art and social texts— social texts that have been pre-digested for their classroom consumption by social workers who call themselves teachers. That's the drift in high school education, insulting as that might sound.

There are all kinds of reasons for that. And I really don't care about them. I only resist them. So there were two reasons, right? Academic respectability: if we're going to do the academic study of cinema, let's do it right. And secondly, it was the only way to take students out of lazy interpretive habits of mind—and take ourselves out of the corresponding lazy understanding that students are already wise. Sorry, I don't think so. I don't think of myself as wise; why would I think of them as wise? What I did think, though, is that if we worked hard at developing a methodology, people would have a richer basis on which to engage in interpretation, which is inevitable and desirable.

The end goal is, in fact, the interpretation of films. Formal analysis is a means to an end. But the end should be postponed for a time. The idea that works of any subtlety or interest are actually subtle and interesting because they say the right things about the world and people in it seems to me immensely naïve and an unproductive way of thinking about it. When I began teaching we had an Athena Analyzer, which is a sixteen-millimetre film projector that would stop frame, go back and go forward to get close-shot analysis, and it became the basis of my teaching. It was also the basis of my graduate experience at New York University. Going through Eisenstein with Annette Michelson shot-by-shot was pretty illuminating. Going through *Psycho* or *Mouchette* with Rothman; Antonioni with Ted Perry. The films got illuminated and were allowed to stand as works of art. It was the same way you'd go through a Giorgione with Panofsky if you were an art student who had such a privilege. It was really the method of Wölfflin. This method spread out across the study of visual arts and came home to roost in the study of another visual art: film.

For me, the films that are worth going back to repeatedly include key figures in the avant-garde cinema. All of that work has a formal dimension, but scholars also study film genres largely through the lens of some version of French structuralism. The genre course also involves issues of narration. And narration is largely understood by formal means, as critics do in literature, right? The models come from French formal critics like Riffaterre and Greimas, from writers like Mieke Bal, who does literary and visual arts analysis. These models have been adapted by people like Edward Branigan and David Bordwell for film study, and these critics announce such openly. So, the formal method has a lot of applications and they actually change how it feels in particular ways—that's what we work on. The idea is to be in the dark with students and work the films in as much detail as we can, either through illustrative passages in films or working through longer stretches. That's the basic teaching method. Sometimes it's super-discursive and sometimes bit-by-bit.

My own teaching otherwise tends to be pretty much lecture-based. I incorporate discussion components, but I'm basically one of those lecture instructors that's never actually relied on the Socratic method as a primary method. I'm too impatient—it's a personality flaw. I admire and envy teachers who are dedicated to the Socratic method. I'm too much in a hurry and I'm really a coverage guy. Like, I'm really anxious for students to get the most variety of films possible. I also trust that the students, when exposed, will be touched by things, inspired by them to do things on their own, and I think that's worked out pretty well. Students who are any good—having any critical imagination and taking the program seriously—eventually go with their own insights and their own ways of putting ideas together. You can tell in their writing. And then every academic program has lots of people who are basically bumps on a log. And the log is floating them toward their degree.

Now, there is always the question of whether an artist knows what he or she is doing, or whether their work was shaped by their biographies (which is a very popular idea in mainstream literary criticism). In film studies, critics are wary of this approach. In the case of filmmakers like Howard Hawks—those who work within a highly organized system like Hollywood or Hong Kong—I don't tend to go to a biographical explanation. It's interesting to know who Howard Hawks is, how he behaved in Hollywood as a personality, but not helpful in grasping his films. Most narrative filmmakers in the classical tradition hide who they are as artists behind their work and at the same time, within the weave of their work, they reveal what it is about their sensibilities that makes them artists. This is easily understood when you realize Hollywood was always deeply suspicious of filmmakers who regarded themselves as more than salaried technicians and how Hollywood took it out on directors like Orson Welles who paraded themselves as artists. It was better to take caution and hide.

On the other hand, I tend to take seriously the statements offered by experimental filmmakers. When you're dealing with Hawks, he'd say, "It was fun to do it that way"—that's pretty much all he has to say. Hitchcock will fulminate on the art of film, but his ideas of "pure cinema" are, to me, another way of hiding himself—even in the book he did with Truffaut. What's interesting about Hitchcock, he does not tell you. When you read Brakhage's *Metaphors on Vision*, you kind of get the sense of the project of an artist, at least the intellectual fictions that he found important to his work.

The same goes for the writings of Maya Deren, Germaine Dulac, Hollis Frampton—these people have produced a significant discourse about their art, and art in general, that we can take seriously. If their thinking constitutes their biography, then yeah, I take their biographies pretty seriously. I have mixed responses when dealing with Antonioni, Kieślowski, Tarkovsky or Tarr—any European art-film figure. In ways, their project is as mysterious to them as it is to us. I don't think Ingmar Bergman knows why he's such an interesting artist and can only articulate himself through his work. Pasolini, well, he says a whole lot of interesting things because he's a really brilliant essayist who gives us insight into his work—and there's a lot of people in between those two.

The critic of English literature feels more often than not that his or her job is to bring Spenser, Chaucer, Shakespeare, Milton alive to the current generation. We should understand that responsibility as a tradition that is centuries old. The philosopher has the same responsibility for Aristotle, Plato, Plotinus, Descartes, Kant. Film is rather odd in that it has a super-truncated history. When does the first artist actually appear in the cinema? Do we want to be super-generous and say Méliès? Or be more restrictive and say Eisenstein? Or are we going to be middle-of-the-road and say it's D.W. Griffith? We're still trying to sort out what it is that might be worth keeping, even as we recognize that pretty much nothing is going to be kept as significant art past the next fifty years.

Cinema is like *sand-painting* (the comparison was Brakhage's). Once it, as a physical matter, disappears... and it's an art that's really tied to a very fragile physical matter. Much more than half of the films made are permanently lost. Our understanding of the hierarchies of the art form—who are the important figures?—that game is doomed and everyone kind of recognizes it. The task of the critic in film is much more melancholy than the task of the critic in literature. The literary critic has reason to believe what they care about will survive. The film critic has a strong suspicion that despite everything,, despite efforts of cinematheques and restorers, we're losing this particular struggle. It's a source of great distress when the study of video games creeps its way in to the study of cinema: it portends that we'll have to move on from cinema to other things that amuse the young. I-don't-care formulations like, "Why are we fetishizing celluloid?" or "Isn't cinephilia, like its name suggests, some kind of pathology?" are all things that suggest to me that everybody's getting ready to abandon the cinema. And that means they're going to be abandoning the artist in the cinema, the idea of preservation for the future.

The critic of the fine arts has the advantage that the things she wishes to understand, to contextualize, are worth gazillions of dollars. Whereas with a film, which has already had its commercial run, is never worth gazillions of dollars. In fact, it's worth very, very little. There's no Christie's for Antonioni prints. The cinema's triumph resulted because it was an art made under the conditions of industrial reproduction. That same historical feature dooms it. There's no film equivalent to an altarpiece in a small village in Italy that turns out to be a masterpiece and gets carted off to a museum in New York. I mean *that's* a fetish object. There might have been a print of *Nosferatu* in a Danish mental hospital—and there was such a discovery twenty years ago—but there could be another in a forgotten cinema basement in Duluth, too.

The art critic can be sure that, barring the collapse of civilization altogether, there can be edition 200 of Doom or Halo and it won't affect the cultural value of that Italian altarpiece. There's some sense in which the moving visual culture will now say, "This is what's happening, baby!" but not Brakhage, Antonioni or Godard. The cinema is coloured by its own obsolescence in visual culture, more so than the already-survived obsolescence of pre-Raphaelite art or the Byzantine icon. "That stuff's gonna live on forever. Well the cinema, *ehn*." As a preserver then, well, I think if you were a student in music and you didn't know Brahms, you'd be deficient. You'd be like a doctor who didn't know what to do with the respiratory system, only what to do with the digestive system. It doesn't make any sense.

In cinema, the view that if you're a kind of accredited film student you should be chasing after the Chris Markers, Antonionis and Eisensteins—that's not really the culture, except among

the few. Instead, it'll be things coming in and out of fashion. So—and I might say this is true of critics generally—film critics generally don't feel a responsibility for the whole thing that film is. And this is worse amongst filmmakers. Filmmakers feel no responsibility for the tradition in which they work. Those who do are exceptional.

Triolet

ITCHY BANG

Indecision faire	Indecision runs
Ceki li envie	Any way it does
Mo senti moi connecter	I'll feel connected to
L'aube pour ene nouvo l'idee	The dawning of a new idea
Li pou vini bientot	Any day now
Pena sentiments	Empty sentiments
Lotte fine arrete	Lotte's off
Prend so medicine	Her meds
Li manque conviction	She lacks conviction
Mais li pu met moi	But she'll cut me
Dans mo place	Down to size
Dans so talon	In her heels
N'importe quand	Any day now
Mo pu sorti	I'll stumble
Dans mo la chambre	Out of this room
Et mo pou dire	And I'll say
Si to refuse tout	If you deny all
L'emotion dans to la vie	The feelings in your life
To formation l'esprit	Your mind's design
Pu dans ene vitrine	Is on display
Si to croire voleur	If you believe

Vivre dans luxe	In the luxury of thieves
Blier qui to doire moi	Forget the debt and what I said
Mo plein dans Triolet	Bored in Triolet
Vieux batiaras pas capav payer	Old fustilugs can't pay
Li paraitre stupide	He looked a stupid thing
So les bas Wolford	In Wolford tights
Et so la chaine en acier	And manacled steel
De toute facon, mo…	Anyway I…
Perce trou dans so la tete	Drilled his head with holes
Enleve tout so tracas	Relieved him of his woes
Bane vagabonds	A press of idlers
Capave detruire to la foi	Can destroy your faith
Dans l'humanite	In humanity
N'importe quand	Any day now
Mo pu sorti de mo cachot	I'll stumble out of this cell
Et mo pu prier	And I'll pray
Si to refuse tout	If you deny all
L'emotion dans to la vie	The feelings in your life
To formation l'esprit	Your mind's design
Pu dans ene vitrine	Is on display
Si to croire voleur	If you believe
Vivre dans luxe	In the luxury of thieves
Blier qui to doire moi	Forget the debt and what I said

All Songs by Kaartikeya Derwish (Mauritian Countryside Plenitude Publishing Company)

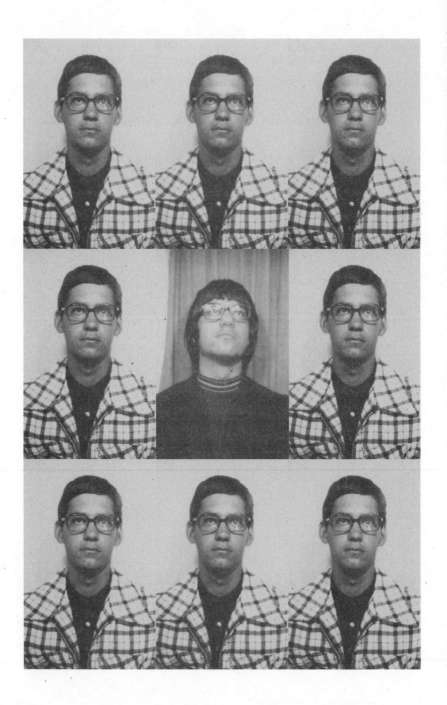

The Slump

JUVENILIA

"Hideous, unfetching—give sense to the feeling, to that muck-heap of judgements a chink of light we can all proudly, not bemusedly, take stock of! If your reader does not understand you, you do not, in a simple manner of speaking, understand your reader. Don't send those searching eyes on me. Direct that reproving gaze inward, to the person that responsibility for such failure is appropriately intended."

For Cornelia, the words provoked sulky outrage. She reached across the table for the jumper she had abandoned earlier, intending to wring it in substitution of Cepecauer's mortar mixer of a neck. She folded in the starfish-like sprawl and remembered the wheedling she'd received from a student named Gyk Zatylny whom she'd met in one of the campus commissaries; Gyk had sung the old man's praises, referring admiringly to the latter's grasp of sublimity and his puzzling brand of peg-legged psychology, the latter of which formed an untoward alignment with the reception aesthetics that had lately fascinated that side of the Atlantic. Compelled in such a way (and if truth be told, hoping to smooth the rough edges of her writing), she had enrolled in the course with eagerness, and even more daringly perhaps, optimism. Realizing now that Gyk's mouth would prove just as fitting a visualization, her fingers tightened around the clump of clothing just as she caught the gaze of the lurching windmill holding the room's attention.

"Cornelia, your disapproval is going to fast become legendary in this classroom if you continue to regard me that way. What is it exactly that you are beginning to... um... take umbrage with? You don't, uh, see the sense of what I'm saying?"

The eight pool floats along Cornelia's line of sight ended their confederated approval with a rubbery shift in bodies that echoed down the spare, almost unmanned room. They looked on expectantly, some with interest, others with panic, unfamiliar with the forms of disfavour that went beyond marking up columns of their notebooks with the despising annotations Cepecauer's body seemed to suggest.

"Well, I can see that you make some very convincing—"

"Because you must realize that what I'm giving you," Cepecauer interrupted, "is the life expectancy... experience you ask of me when you walk through those doors. Who's in the mood for an anecdote? When my ex-wife read my first book, she strained her neck to look at me—her way of condemning the vanity of my scribblings, you see. Very melodramatic, this woman, suffering in the womb, like. 'Ronald,' she would say. For emphasis, saying my name as if it had one syllable: '*Runld*, one of our marriage—or this pitiful reflection of it—will survive this trespass because I cannot live with the idea of sharing a bed with a purveyor of such colourless...' Something along those high-flown lines. Anyway, I was within my rights when I told the arch-witch she wasn't exactly helping me weigh the alternatives. If she'd spent half the time normally wasted on repining at the gym, well... Somewhere—don't ask me where—it is said that literature is supposed to double your pleasure, like having a frig alongside a mirror; alas, the only thing a reflection ever doubled on that bloated sow was from the waist down… What was I saying? My options were very easy, though limited, even before weighing them. I'm getting sidetracked. I can tell you can tell."

Cepecauer paused for effect. "Therefore, I sold ten thousand copies of my book. Hardly a hard sell—the decision I mean, not the book! The point being, not exactly to the contrary of what you may be thinking—put your hand down, Cornelia— that you can in fact change a horse in midstream—again, not the book. Also, that sometimes conviction, persistence—such qualities as can only take you so far—are not enough in this dogsy-dog world. Personal sacrifice alone will not see you the rest of the way through." He turned his back to the class, the rancorous angling of his shoulders directed at one person alone. "In your cases, the humility that is entailed by the positioning of your seats."

The day ended with a sense of defeat Cornelia was stiff-lipped about preventing, even if it came at the cost of the self-possession by which she abided. She felt as if her body had been unsettled by Cepecauer's appearance, his suggestive pointing when alluding to former lovers working a similarly lament-able magic over her imagination. It was better to envision the last three hours of her life having been enacted in a dumb show so that dignities could be preserved, stomachs left unchurned. A victory would have meant countering Cepecauer with the scores of objections normally advanced in the face of such blustering, though she immediately realized the futility of the endeavour.

The mere thought of sharing anything in common with a scurrilous blatherer—even something as incidental as oppos-ite sides of an argument—made her reach for the starry hollow of the sky. Imagining the hideous conflation of their limbs and faces, the spider-child of their synchronous minds, wrought as much chaos over her as the idea of their disentanglement; the way Cepecauer droned on about "sharing byways" with a reader, "toiling and moiling with a companion fair," provoked other hopeless imaginings, and she recognized that such assignment-returning overtures would always come burdened with the honorary reader's own outmoded sensibilities. Her biggest fear was Cepecauer handing back a writing sample in the future, sputtering a winking eyeball in her direction while proclaiming: "Fine work, Darteris. Very fine. *Could* have set it better myself if I tried." Or alternately: "Fine work, Darteris. Very fine. *Couldn't* have set it better myself if I tried."

Cornelia vowed never to read Cepecauer's work because the fear of his influence was too great, looming large like a winding sheet. He had been, Gyk avowed, something of a phenomenon in the past, a glory-lapper who wished to slip in between the cracks left unused by more capable writers and who had succeeded in that role due in no small part to assiduity. He allied himself with the Rough Gruffs who spoke with disaffection about the opposite sex, exploring their literary bodies in terms of how parts were proportioned in relation to each other, sexual compliance somehow ridiculously deriving from those arrangements. Such writers referred to the female form as a gamesman makes reference to a trampoline, describing the exact degree it would resist or admit human force, and using the same caddish terminology in which such athletes are wont to dabble in their ignoble kingdom of sport: the mangy, disease-ridden street corner. Gyk had even once related how Cepecauer's novel *The Honeysuckle Fleet* vainly attempted to ennoble the figure of the onanist as a tortured repentant, frustrating his climax so as not to sully the stature of his revered object of arousal.

This circumspection around Cepecauer, however second-hand in its acquisition, was in some respects justified. It was true that he came loaded with false promises, but it was also accurate that as an esteemed novelist, his talents could undoubtedly prove beneficial in some vague, presently undetermined way. A semester's worth of doddering writer's intuition had to come at a cost, and only by enrolling could Cornelia find out if its value would be offset by a writerly provincialism.

Cornelia's mind returned to the fateful present. She briskly gathered her things, made her exit from the classroom, and stepped outside where the brackish air felt rough on her uncovered arms. She saw Cepecauer head off in another direction and felt relieved to walk untroubled and without evasions. The sight of her college commons room soon occasioned another return to old thoughts though, this time to the exact moment when Gyk had successfully overcome her reservations about the course.

"Gyk, it's altogether simple," she had emphasized plainly. "What have I to learn cooped up in a class that on the face of it serves as the glorification of a living man's reputation? The extravagance of the idea! Let me guess. How to end all of my stories with henpecked men? No, better yet, with snipe hunts! There are some people who can't stand to admit failure when it's staring them blankly in the face."

Gyk had stifled a laugh. "It sounds silly when you say it like that."

"My saying it has nothing to do with it sounding silly. What I want to know is if breezing through them is in any way relevant."

"I should think so. When you hear what I think they're about, or what's potentially worse, of what actually happens in them, you're inclined to believe that it's all this twaddle about money being the easiest thing in the world to come by next to standing downwind of a woman's temper, of finding a job you can't bear or how a man's access to sex is like his access to a good deli. But there's beauty in those stories as well—albeit shame too—which is what makes it so unoriginal to want to dog pile."

"Then I imagine the experience is likely to bore me. Isn't learning how to make the same mistakes as a man inclined to view them as triumphs a problem for you? He'd be of practically no use to me unless he retracted every word he'd ever published, and he's not liable to do any such thing. I think considering enrolment has been a miserable error in judgement."

"Pshaw! That's an irrational fear if I ever heard one. Won't be the outcome of attending a few classes—writing like him, I mean. It's not like you go on talking to me and expect to assume my feelings on any matter. It's quite the reverse, what with you being so headstrong. You know he's starting a new imprint with his publisher, don't you? You never know with these things, might lead to something promising. In any event, what you'd be going for is his input on your work—if it's in fit condition with publishing standards."

"I know what passes these days for standards, Gyk, and it has nothing to do with being published."

The couple had then rounded a curve along the walk of the college's main building and tramped their way through the mutinous stork's bills that girdled the bronze war memorial outside Cedar Hall. As they rushed swiftly past the surge of students near the entry doors, Cornelia almost failed to notice Cepecauer amid the maelstrom of tumbling bodies, a wiry gravel bar defiantly standing his ground.

"If he knew those standards," Cornelia continued, "wouldn't you think he'd be at home slogging away on a book making good on that knowledge rather than wasting it on us? Why am I always so suspicious of those who are in a position to instruct what they so ineptly cannot put to good use?"

"Sour grapes are always in season."

She had looked away from Gyk's face for a moment only to see Cepecauer hunched awkwardly over some papers. Cepecauer looked up and locked onto a face he instantly recognized. Unaccustomed to resisting opportunities to discuss his favourite subject, he'd stuffed his notes away into his briefcase and outstretched a friendly hand to Gyk from thirty feet away.

"Gyklny, good to see you, my half-caste friend. Who's this with you?"

"Hello, Mr. Cepecauer. We were just discussing the 'Death, Dying and Age' course you're teaching next semester. My friend here is of two minds about enrolling."

Cornelia imagined what Gyk's mouth attempting to devour itself would look like.

"She's real keen on the subject matter," Gyk continued. "But wants to know what your writing's like. It's been a challenge just to put into words."

Cepecauer, whose skin was already of such an unnatural pallor that one had only to guess where the blood had drained to, appeared here to become agitated with the recognition conferred upon him. His fingers made odd contortions, recalling strands of a shag carpet weighed down with dampness. When the twisting fit had passed, the author had curved his lips like a pair of sweeping legs and combed his fingers through his grimy hair, as if such movements were acknowledged signs of thoughtfulness—such were the images Cornelia had tabulated to memory before he made his dramatic pronouncements on the life cycle of mankind as it related to a meaningless existence.

"It'll all depend on what you want out of this course, Miss..." he began, hoping to be introduced formally. "Whether or not the value that I have to offer is of any use for your purposes. Have you read my work? No? It'd be a good idea if you did, particularly my last two books—the strongest of the lot. They're good, great, some are even accustomed to say. I think you'll enjoy them, provided you don't misunderstand them—their intention that is. You'll get a feeling of what it is I'm trying to do in this course, what I'm trying to get the young to rub up against. Zatylny here realizes, er, has realized that, haven't you?"

"On the whole of it you could say as m—"

"Yes, I really think that you'd stand to gain quite a bit. Quite a lot, by rights. You know, perhaps I can speak to something that may be of interest to you. Have you ever considered where the impulse to write comes from? Yes, a young South Asian authoress like yourself surely has. Well, I hope you're not too flummoxed when I tell you that I in nowise can begin to discover why! Ho ho, not what you were quite expecting, I'll wager. But I'll have you know, the mark of a prime artist, the real capital thinker, like—is absolute ignorance in the face of inspiration's ultimate cause. The more forthright the avowal, the more towering a force. I know no more as to the nature of this native compulsion than of the revolutions of the earth. It isn't the writer's domain to discover his own motivations, and it certainly isn't for others when he heaves over the horizon. I tell my young authorlings not to brook any attempts at such a thing. It's dreadful and uncalled for. You cannot exist as both the bloody mirror and the mirrored; you can communicate with each other, and establish symmetries of passion, but you cannot be in two places at once, now can you? Simple, fundamental physics—the 'science of nature,' that. And I hope to expedite neither your understanding and most certainly not your fascination in both of these ludicrous objectives, so you should not expect as much from my class."

Cepecauer's handle on the authorial purpose appeared superficially justified, much like the elbow-patched sports jacket he'd finally found reason enough to drape around his lowered shoulders, now that he was in good moral standing to be in the company of men and women half his age. His movements were a graceless performance; he never seemed to look anyone in the eye, but instead seemed to be concentrating on some distant and probably unidentified vanishing point located directly above one's hairline. He had finished droning nineteen to the dozen and hitching his pants around his bulging paunch, whereupon he finally bent his eyes at Cornelia, as if awaiting an answer to an unvoiced query.

"Wh... what books will we be reading, Mr. Cepecauer?" Cornelia stammered. "Can I ask what aspect of death we'll be touching on?"

"I won't be... I won't be the one directing the attention of the class toward those particulars. It's a very organic composition— the students that is. That will be your responsibility, assuming you enrol. I'm interested to know what facets of dying are of most interest to you. We'll be exploring these subjects primarily through your writing. Workshops, lots and lots of workshops for the journeymen... women. They'll be neither watch nor ward for bad writing in my course, dearie. As for books, should we use any at all, I'm undecided for the moment. Some of the greats will be accounted for too, perhaps. It would make sense, however, to include some of the forthcoming books from my new imprint at Dowley—advanced reader copies anyway. We're thinking of calling it *Oratorian*—books meant to be read aloud, cover to cover. We've really got some dynamic voices in the offing. Not a European man in the lot. I'm merely editing it, you see. It's going to do a lot for these writers, going to ruffle all the feathers that need ruffling. We'll be a beacon to light the future, put some of these decrepit gaffers in their place. I'll let Mr. Gyklny here fill in the gaps, though. I can't tarry too long I'm afraid, run off my feet. And some manuscripts..."

He trailed off at that point and then was gone, something setting him off in the direction of the north quadrant where the university's wavering boundary appeared to trade furtive architectural insults against tumbledown restaurants and Hammer Horror grocers' shops. Cornelia had often considered how in such an imagined confrontation the university would prove unwilling to utter any of its imprecations to the array of businesses along the opposite end of Main Street openly; it instead dispatched such stratally ambiguous individuals like Cepecauer to deliver its rumbling salvos in the form of his refusals to leave those establishments or his penchant for exclusively reading campus periodicals while patronizing them. Who exactly was leading such a war of rearranged personnel remained unclear: a renewed stream of students found steady employment along this strip annually, while the university never succeeded in dispatching Cepecauer with finality, making a calculation of gains and losses impossible to determine.

These recollections now informed the agency of Cornelia's feet. The young student discovered her drifting had become a semi-plotted course for the Brisket House—the deli Cepecauer frequented—a destination for which she cursed her stomach as well as her head. She hesitated at the door, knowing her instructor was accustomed to capping his lectures with Cobb Clubs and burnt coffee. Perhaps some revered master of the craft had done the same and he believed the transference of professional ability effected by a digestive medium? The post office was just a few metres away, and Cornelia thought it better to avoid the deli so close to her class finishing.

Her weekly visits to the post had begun six months ago when she was unceremoniously rubbed out of a low-paying position at a publishing house where she weeded through manuscripts. Things had come to a pretty pass when a senior editor named Edgar Nishimura managed to stop cheques from being mailed out, inventing "vacationing bookkeepers" and giving false assurances of their arrival to palliate his employees' tactical prodding. The situation deteriorated to such a degree that Cornelia found herself penning impassioned letters to members of parliament in the hopes that they would be scandalized to hear of the practices of skint businessmen; that her efforts curtailed all progress on her own novel did not trouble her, such was the intensity of her outrage. When Cornelia was turned out on her ear for her manoeuvrings, she remained undaunted to the prospect of getting even, having devised a scheme that needed comparatively little effort—all it required was some "light treading on the boards," in a manner of speaking.

Upon entering the post office, Cornelia approached a side-table and extracted some stationery she carried in her messenger bag. She rifled through the six letters packed away that morning and paused to decide which note would unsettle Nishimura more. Each letter contained a continuation of some dilemma more distressing than the last, broken off into instalments and written under various aliases, soliciting in some miraculous way a devoted correspondence. Cornelia considered whether the dying lost half-brother bidding a tearful farewell or the feted author with allegations of stolen material would cause more harm. Recalling the encouraging response toward a brotherly meeting and the obliging assurances of sorting out any legal entanglements caused by oversight, the plucky writer posted both missives and began to rush out the door, as if loitering at the scene of the crimes, such as they were fast becoming, would prove imprudent.

Just then, wearing a vermilion jumper and carrying a large envelope between his blotchy fingers that evidently contained a manuscript, Cepecauer entered the office and announced himself to the occupants by clearing his throat obnoxiously. Cornelia stood stock still and tried her best to conceal her appearance. In doing so, she forgot the four remaining letters held snugly between her hands.

"Hello again, Cornelia. I can tell that you're going to kick yourself later for not asking, so I'll get it out of the... It's my new book—managed in between lectures and office hours if you can believe it. Something called a *roman à clef* I was told expofactus. Not entirely harebrained if the application is in earnest, what? Possibly an Oratorian book, possibly not. Would that be unethical, I wonder? That's exactly the sort of thing that

I'm lacking—a kind of internal barometer for moral transgression. Would come in handy, that. My very own Zhang Chongren, an Alene Lee by my side. We could call it an ethics officer. But what would the salary for something like that entail, I wonder?" Cepecauer nudged a finger into his ear, foiling the blockage that irritated him, but without bothering for once to inspect its contents. He instead directed it to Cornelia's four remaining envelopes. "Well, there's coincidence for you. How do you know Edgar? I'm mailing him myself."

Cornelia's eyes widened behind swollen hoops of light, a trick of her glasses' positioning beneath the ceiling track bulbs which she hoped concealed her start from the recognition. The envelopes in her hands were facing him. She'd readied stories to offer in the event of being cornered in the post office, but none of these paranoid contingencies accounted for her interlocutor knowing her ex-employer first-hand. "Our Edgar? E... Ed and I go back a ways."

"So I gather. But *how* do you know him?"

"P... print. Print industry. Mainly."

"Yes, buggerlugs works for Dowley & Hamm. Has for ages." Cepecauer refused to budge, waiting for an answer even if it meant a noncommittal one. The thought of genuflection sickened her, but avoiding an honest reply helped brace herself for what followed.

"That's your new novel, you said?" she asked. "You'll be sending it off to Edgar I assume?"

"Ah, no. Not directly. His strengths don't exactly lie in reading, but one must pay respects to the gatekeeper and his portcullis."

The confessionary nature of the admission caught her off-balance, but emboldened her for the remainder of the dialogue. "He has his days," Cornelia offered. "He surprises even the most cynical of selves."

Cepecauer scrutinized her face; apparently satisfied, he continued his line of gibing, even past the point of carelessness. "Look, there's no point in being charitable to lost causes. Edgar's place is in managing other editors. He's a pencil-pusher who cavilled his way to the top. But if you ask me the last time he read a book, let alone took an interest in one, I'd say I'd rather my afternoon go unspoiled. Five hundred?"

"Five hundred what?"

"Dollars. For the ethics officer. You've got those in spades. You keep me in check in the classroom, don't you know?"

"I'm not sure. Edgar had something akin to an ethics officer, but the duties as I understood them were largely ceremonial. That might not be the right word for it. They primarily did other things, and didn't hold the title as you put it."

"Think it over. The position, I mean. We can discuss remuneration at another time. Are you working on anything? I don't think we have a writer from the Orient yet. For Oratonian—it's on my list. We have a map with pins in it at the office. Something to consider, if you have anything you want to send my way."

"I may have something."

"Are you keeping well in my class? Are you getting what you bargained out of it?"

"I suppose I won't have an answer for you until we've actually submitted assignments. It's a real twister, the one you've assigned."

Cepecauer removed a sleek black briar from his breast pocket, but realizing his situation, thought better of it. He extinguished the match against his finger and winced. It was enough that Cornelia had witnessed the token of refinement. He'd come up hard, this one, obviously; hard enough to know which blamed pipe would get people looking at you in a certain way.

"You've encouraged recommendations from us," Cornelia continued. "So I thought it would be within order if I suggested something. Would it be worthwhile if you wrote the assignment with us? I know it's unorthodox, but I think that with you leading the pack, as it were, we'd all gain a better understanding of some of those 'cultivations of humanity' you endearingly make mention of. That way we could see where we've been going wrong."

"Culti… so you have been listening! Yes, that sounds arrangeable. But the others, some of the dimmer ones, I'm not so sure they'd be as receptive, that they'd approve. They may talk, begin to think that I'm involved… involving myself too much."

"Oh no. No, no, no, Mr. Cepecauer. I've spoken with the class and they're very keen on the idea. It was all a matter of who would get to you first to broach the subject." Her palms began to perspire at the lie, thinking on what the worst possible outcomes would be, not *if* but *when* Cepecauer found out she'd led him by the nose.

"It's the perfect timing for it, actually. I've just gotten this load off my shoulders, and it would be the clinch as to what I'm to do next. Everything turned to good use. The past six months have been such a bitter run of corrections and excisions that some actual writing would be a tall order, though a welcomed one. You know, I think I will commit to it. Give you something I wish I'd had when I was wet behind the ears."

Cornelia hardly believed she'd earwigged the clod into believing her—her disbelief was enough to tune out the rest of the Slump's conversation, as she had christened him to no one but herself. It would be worth more than a laugh—something to add to his locomotion of ridiculous philosophies. Only now there would be confirmation of his benign stupidity, an article of correction to apply against his chuntering, mind-clubbing fuzziness.

"That's wonderful!" she interrupted without giving thought to what he was saying. "Very sportsmanlike of you. And maybe it'll be of use to you, writing on a subject that seems to have captivated your imagination for so long." A stab in the dark, having still abstained from looking at his work.

"Yes, you're right on that count. Never a wasted opportunity to play the sophisticate. You know, my agent told me that was the way to go, yammering away on the same subject but from various angles for years and years. Improve my standing."

This avowal of hackery, seemingly free of ironical touches of any kind, demonstrated that Cepecauer believed honesty in the face of any delusion, no matter how horrifying a quality at which to be admitted, was the sort of achievement that would celebrate his name. He would, so to speak, rather continue wading through a pool of quicksand, admitting in the process that he'd neglected to guard against a concealed depression lying ahead, than avoid the deathly entrapment altogether by bothering to look where one foot settled after the other. Such was the rationale of the cretin, doing more for the safekeeping of his mental constitution than the prospect of a safe rescue. His problem, she initially thought, had lain in the inherited understandings and rootless experience that was generally traded among sciolists to stave off extinction; Cornelia had chalked up his thoughts on writing to an outmoded perspective. She now realized the terrible error. The man was legitimately blocked, no two, three ways about it.

After their conversation ended, Cornelia lamely took leave of Cepecauer and returned to her home to start her assignment. It proved her first legitimate attempt at composition since leaving Dowley & Hamm that wasn't motivated chiefly by vengeance, and even then, most of the assignment's contents were appropriated from Nishimura's own unbosomed emotionality that Cornelia's petitions had successfully aroused.

The first class after the weekend proved a surprising one for Cornelia's classmates who were welcomed with copies of Cepecauer's abbreviated meditations on love and death. The students did not usually speak to one another, preferring a coded system of glances to indicate bewilderment instead. Today proved an exception and solicited a few titters in the class, concealed only by the buzzing within Cepecauer's throat which indicated boobish satisfaction. Cornelia took her place among the other classmates, fetching her assignment from a file folder. Aware that the time had finally come to confront the fear that, as an accomplished writer of some modest renown, Cepecauer's writing might actually appeal to her, she looked to the neatly arranged document before her with now only a minimal amount of dread.

It doesn't pay to get mixed up with your pupils. No.

A flash of relief swept over her.

It doesn't.

Her eyes, inured by Nishimura's training to evaluate its style and embellishments, for once sped along the pages to assess the basic components of the plot.

It doesn't pay, those feelings of vernal exhilaration, in the heartland of dynamic emotional upheavals, the weight you finally manage to keep off (all that Din-intel), the arousal of smooth, smacking flesh and lapped stomachs congregating in the grip of a Brandy Alexander hangover. Why me? (Why not me?) I ask myself over and over and over and over and over as I count the seconds before I climax. Life, ever mysterious, remains even more mysterious for the uninitiated foreigner. She is forty years my junior and I just don't seem to care. Did I ever?

The short story concerned a young woman enrolled in an MFA program with a prominent writer who initiated a flirtation that quickly evolved into a forbidden love affair, seduced no less by the author's "creative fearlessness." The piece went to great pains to extol the virtues of the student's body and rail against the university's unfashionable views on such relationships, which the narrator attributed to some sort of undiagnosed complex preoccupied with sexual meddling. The student bore a vague resemblance to Cornelia, but could very well have been mistaken for any of the other women in the classroom at the moment. She regarded her assignment with fortitude, which despite reservations about its title and execution, comforted her. Her piece bore no resemblance to the monstrosity Cepecauer had managed to give voice, flesh and form.

This was the final straw with Gyk, who had proved himself both in his capacity of Cepecauer's white-haired boy and defender, not to mention a rather undependable friend, more outstandingly incompetent than usual. A cloud of chalk dust sailed into the air as Cepecauer rubbed his hands together to marshal the attention of the class to the board, where he had written the words *voice* and *you* in large letters, connected by a branching double arrow pointing in opposite directions.

"I have heard your summons class," Cepecauer boldly intoned. "Willingly do I accept its terms." He looked into the hard faces of his listeners, but the sad fool could not find his challenger, much less the spark of his galvanized affections.

T. BALTUCH

Swiddenworld: Selected Correspondence with Tabitha Gotlieb-Ryder

GOLDIE'S VAN DONGEN

To SERGE MAYACOU, *of* HAMILTON

SERGE,

I made some serious enquiries on your behalf about whether Goldie would be amenable to selling the Paul Kirchner and Peter van Dongen pieces. Kirchner is a definite no; with van Dongen, although he is rather attached to it, he did assure me somewhat indeterminately that this would not be the case forever. "This is *not* an 'anfractuous' enticement to entertain offers"—(his exact choice of words). I don't know that he has a firm number in mind; when he says something like that, it's usually to weigh up whether it's enough incentive to let it go. If it's too low, he may not counter-offer, just respond, "I'd rather just keep it" (as he has done before).

Confidentially speaking, however, I think I can tell you that no one—at least while I have been in his employ—has ever made an offer for it, much less expressed so much as an interest. I don't want to get your hopes up, but I think this bodes well. I know that he has been negotiating for years with a collector in Kalamazoo about an original Roy G. Krenkel. Goldie is under the impression that they are about to agree on a number (seven years onwards), but this wouldn't be the first time that he's overestimated finances, or his bargaining power for that matter. Don't let appearances to the contrary fool you—though the studio is certainly spacious, well-situated (opulent some might even be accustomed to say)—Le Nid de Duc it is not. I have your contact information now, so I can advise you should the time come.

I enjoyed our conversation about Bruce Pennington and *Eschatus*. I am not aware of any publisher other than Paper Tiger ever having rights to publication through legitimate means, however. You are always welcome to stop by in the studio if you have any further questions, or simply want to look through what Goldie will be putting up for sale in the future—I would be more than happy to set anything (available) aside for you.

–T. Gotlieb-Ryder

To T.G.R., *of* TORONTO

TABITHA,

Thank you for your note. I am touched by the gesture of consideration. I enjoyed making your acquaintance as well—if you could reach out should the van Dongen go to market, I would be in your happy debt. I would not hesitate to show my gratitude.

I looked through my *Galaxies* and could not believe you were able to reference the artist based on my inadequate methods of description. I can confirm it was Phillipe Caza who did the cover in question.

–S. Mayacou

To SERGE MAYACOU, of HAMILTON

SERGE,

Movement on the Krenkel front imminent. If all goes as planned, the transaction will be finalized within a day or two. Privately, I can confirm Goldie is still taken with the van Dongen (it currently resides over his mantelpiece, next to the portraiture his wife Marlana made in his likeness). He will push lesser pieces on you to generate immediate funds for the Krenkel deal; additionally, he took note of your interest in Virgil Burnett and Howard Sherman (your taste does you credit) and has pieces in his possession to which he no longer bears an attachment. If you push past his resolve for the van Dongen, and make no allusions to possessing an awareness of privileged information, I know for a fact he will capitulate.

–T. Gotlieb-Ryder

To T.G.R., of TORONTO

TABITHA,

The van Dongen is at the framers now. If I am being perfectly honest, I am still shaking with disbelief at my good fortune of having come into contact with you. Not the crown jewel by any stretch, but a very good specimen of the man's untrammelled control of static movement, and a happy resident in any serious collection. What I find most appealing is how it is an example of his more oppressive and rough line work, uncluttered with the pretenses of Swartean flatness. I hope I am not being too forward in the hope of wanting you to see where it will be eventually situated at my residence. Please allow me to treat you to dinner one night as a show of my appreciation.

–S.

To SERGE MAYACOU, of HAMILTON

SERGE,

That would be lovely. When will you next be in the city? I leave all particulars to you, and can be free most evenings after Goldie has closed the gallery. I thought it would be worth mentioning that he has recently made contact with a reputed former associate of Frank R. Paul who has a small stockpile of his artwork. The provenance is currently being assessed by someone in Teaneck. Interest is expected to be above average/crash-hot on account of renewed interest in his work; knowing Goldie's pricing, this will thin out the competition considerably. I can bring stats to dinner if you don't object.

–Tabby

THE JOY BEAUT LOVER AND THE GLITZ CUNT

To T.G.R., of TORONTO

MY LITTLE FUCKLING,

You were a right saucy Glitz Cunt last night. Nail on the ready, I could not wait to have you bucking and frisking like a hind in the wind. Your blithesome bunghole and its raucous puckerings hypnotized my mind to the Omega Point—glossolalic pronouncements, keeping perfect time with your intoxicated breathing, the echoing singsong of your colliding juddlies recalling me from the distant heavens of your tantra, the hint of a fetid musk wafting from your armpits. A more debauch ritornello has not been heard this side of midnight when I let my gasps unroll into moans.

When you began reciting the names of the assured masters—"Rey Feibush, Alex Schomburg, Virgil Finlay, Don Ivan Punchatz"—while engaged in unholy congress, I barely had the sense to blunder out myself into your mouth before it was too late. Even if I wanted to, I could not dispel the image of you soothingly anointing my gonads with my seed. My sweetest Tabby, tell me you will let me have you again, that you are not over-boyed (and with whom I must vie for your attentions). Barring such circumstances, that you will see me again in whatever capacity that allows me access to your naked splendour— cockservant, witness, figger, what have you. Let me be your nightstick, I have no hard limits. Old guard leather need not apply.

–The Joy Beaut Lover

To SERGE MAYACOU, of HAMILTON,

DEAREST WHORELET,

Did you think to have satisfied my ravening desires, O cockless wonder? Did I say you were finished with me? Did I give you permission to finish before I told you to? Your anointment was merely a prelude to your despoiliation. The sequelae of your actions will be tenfold. We will fructify your ten-a-penny cock yet, drudge. The acccidulants in your jissom will smart and stain your body, your mouth, your anus—I can hardly wait to see how much farther I can claw my finger up your gate and have you glimpse the storms in heaven. We will make a *swidden* out of you yet. Once we have finished laying the groundwork for your vitiation, I will sanctify your cockling with an appropriate and fitting ranking. I dub my quim Apeslayer: violator of all who kneel before my bilious heat. Fie, swoon and tremble before my blessed chalice, sate yourself on the quiniferous piquancy of my urticating clunge.

Do you know Julius Leblanc Stewarts' work? *Nymphs Hunting*? Our pairing brings it to life. Familiarize yourself with its sick-making majesty. I will brook no clanking irons. Does it bring you shame or pride that you fuck for profit? You are a grotty, foul, lob-sided cock-disaster who can't make up his mind about which hole you want to screw any more than you can decide which gets you hotter, the possibility that I might have an Ohrai or a Mark Harrison in the wings, hidden from Goldie's view. Poor, lamentable art lover, born too late to get in on the ground floor of Guido Crepax's reputation being pulled out of the rot-funk of the Italian gutter... You need me to derrick the vicissitudes of the art market so that I can maximize the length and breadth of your dollars like I maximize the length and breadth of your meat when I guide you inside me. I own you, therefore I can unmake you. You will need a shuftiscope when I am done with you, worm—skinfuls of foof,

–Glitz Cunt

To T.G.R., *of* TORONTO

TABBY,

I read your letter with anticipation in the stockroom at work. I was already hard before my fingers found their way around my member. I frigged myself quickly and wiped myself on your letter before licking it dry. Your mention of Crepax occasioned my memory on the pages I had let slip all these years—Sterankos, Bodēs, Morrows. Why must you demean me so? Have I not been a percipient if tolerable servitor? What can I do to prove the fealty I swear unto you and your crimson cathedral of smut, bunt and disease? I could write a vexillology of your red minge and the congregants who advance behind it. The mild fragrance of sweat admixing with the sour sluices of your asshole awaken a dormant pathology inside me, the shit-stink of your soul are like embers that make your twat bawl out "Decretals of Minge!" in farting whimpers.

My waking reveries of your sour stockinged feet pressed against my nose while I nibble on the flaking skin of your heels prevents me from coordinating the movement of my legs when I am returning from the bar. Just the other night I sat drunk, transfixed on another woman's legs who reminded me of yours— they had the same bandiness, I swear I could perceive the same sweat stink of your armpits and the same contumelious smirk on your lips. I had a good frig with my thighs and had enough baby batter spilling down my ankles that I lost sense of myself and delighted in pouring my porter over my lap just so the barmaid could pat me down with her dirty dish rag.

I made my way home in a skronking stupor, vomited in the stairwell, and began to unbutton my shirt and trousers so that

I could feel something warm on my chest and groin. I could not manage much more than half my normal size (it looked like a pufterlooner) but I smeared some vomitus up myself all the same and began to see the emblazoned image of your red, inflamed bunghole in my mind's eye, the raphe extending down your taint like Jacob's Ladder. When I had recomposed myself, I made my way into my apartment and called you on the telephone. We discussed Hannes Bok and Rowena Morrill briefly, but ended our conversation abruptly because you were feeling poorly. I regained my composure shortly afterwards and fell asleep while *Charlie Bubbles* was playing on the television.

    –The Welland Canal

INSUFFLATION TAKES TWO

To SERGE MAYACOU, *of* HAMILTON

SERGE,

I have not heard from you for several weeks now; a third letter going unanswered is bordering on incivility, but I think I catch your meaning. I could forgive your remissness if I did not suspect an ulterior motive. Did I frighten you? I warned you that my sex was not for the meek and faint-hearted. Did the insufflation of your nethers break you? Did you not like the feeling of being entered and roiled from within? Did the mere sight of blood make the measure of a man burrow up inside you?

You'll have no bitter tears from I, worm-feeding cock-spastic. Never set foot in my place of business then; never write me, never phone me. I hope your van Dongen turns out to be a fake—knowing Goldie, the truth isn't that far off. No one will deign engage you in transactions—your collecting days are finished. You'll bear the mark of a welch in our circle, which I can assure you, is as broad as my mouth. Good luck ever getting into the pants of anyone else who knows who Bernard Sachs is. I hope you get gonorrhea in your throat and crust scabies in your taint, you hypospadic pup. Your necessaries smell like a leper colony. You were pissed up against a wall and hatched in the sun!

It's a cock sweetie, not a crumpled bill you're trying to squeeze into a vending slot. Fuck off and die you grostulating, rent-a-cock choirboy! The Glitz Cunt is dead!

To T.G.R., of TORONTO

TABITHA,

I know full well that I am the last person you expected to hear from again, but I can only hope that if you are still reading these words, a morbid curiosity will give you the inclination to understand what I have to say.

Let me start by saying that I cannot apologize enough for my determined efforts to ignore you: yes, as I'm sure it will come as no surprise, I admit it freely. I was compelled to sever our relationship, such as I believe it was fast becoming, from outside influences I felt forced to succumb to. I will spare no detail, because I believe that an orderly mind still counts for something in these days of ease.

A few days after our last telephone conversation, I received a summons to Goldie's Treffan Court offices. He refused to elaborate on the nature of the visit, save to say that it would concern a matter of "renewable interest." I was met immediately by Goldie and two individuals approximately in their forties bearing the waxen demeanours of mortuary attendants. I believe you will know them to be Ms. Runthenthorpe and Mr. Freleng, celebrated art-scoundrel muckety-mucks and long-time associates of Goldie. They had a proposition for me, which piqued my interest, knowing their reputation for implacable, purposeful acquisition.

Runthenthorpe had gathered that I was making moves to acquire several Murphy Anderson pieces as privately as possible and almost always through direct sales. Freleng, similarly, had become aware of the growing Howard Sherman collection I was amassing. This unsettled me to no end as I had taken considerable steps to remain anonymous and to never discuss the pieces publicly unless someone demonstrated the velleity to relinquish a piece. The more publicity these transactions had, the better chance potterers would come hunting for the sake of the muck and unsettle my own motivations of unspoiled, artistic contemplation, as we have discussed in days of yore.

Goldie and co. asked me in no uncertain terms if I would be willing to place bets at a coming auction they were holding. I professed that I did not quite grasp their meaning. Freleng and Runthenthorpe were in the process of downsizing their respective collections and were feeling anxious that they would not recoup their original expenditure, or that their pieces would not fetch the prices that in their estimation the broader marketplace could secure. It dawned on me that they were asking me to engage in shill bidding. I did not make any moral calculations on this front, but briefly considered the repercussions if caught. Goldie assured me that the only people who knew of the arrangement were present in the room, and that it had been the first time that any of them had attempted anything of the sort. A "chanson des mouches," Goldie had called it. He opined that though ants and bees were like communists, flies comprehended private enterprise consummately.

Before I could ask what would motivate me to assume the risk, Freleng and Runthenthorpe produced Anderson and Sherman originals from their respective collections. I was besotted with the Sherman in particular because I had assumed the majority of these pages had been destroyed at the production level long ago. Goldie assured me I could have one artwork on the spot, and the other at the end of the auction. If things went according to plan, they envisioned a time when I could call on them to perform the same service, ensuring a provident future. We shook on the agreement cordially, and then Runthenthorpe and Freleng took their leave of us, placing the Sherman on the escritoire by the entrance door for me to wrap up.

When we were alone, Goldie took the Sherman in his hands to appraise the detail with the assistance of a magnifying glass before asking me how I knew about the van Dongen. I feigned ignorance as to his meaning, for he still did not suspect the nature under which I acquired it. I don't need to tell you that van Dongen's work experienced a significant uptick in the months since Goldie off-loaded the page, essentially tripling in value virtually overnight. Goldie harboured some ill will on this front, but was more impressed than anything by my talents for prognostication. I attempted to disabuse him of this opinion, but he was fixated, especially since my artistic interests overlapped with those of Runthenthorpe and Freleng.

The matter was settled that he wanted me as a junior buyer and assistant. The suggestion was both attractive and dismaying—

this was essentially the position you held with him. I balked at the offer as graciously as I could. He would not take "no" for an answer, however. He didn't care if I had heard of the Kupferstichkabinett or not; merely that I had produced results. He laid out exciting terms for my employment, but insisted that my focus could never attenuate or he would seek a replacement (a credo, as I would learn, he had lived by for years). Goldie found your focus recently to be lacking, and your oversight concerning the van Dongen was uncommonly galling to him. Of course, I am to be held accountable for the so-called lapses in your discernment.

It was inside the probable that your professional relationship with Goldie was now at an end. My intent was to continue seeing you and to work for Goldie, maximizing my wits and connections to more than make up for what had befallen you by my hand. It was my hope to buy you an original Pennington as a preliminary token of contrition. Your first letter had arrived asking why I had not responded to you, and though I drafted a version of the letter you now hold in your hands, I lost my nerve to send it. Goldie's disobliging work expectations occupied the best of me for a few days, and by then it was too late, for your last letter had arrived on my doorstep making the decision easy for me. I was soon filled with tremendous sorrow and regret— you seemed perfectly adamant (and within your right) to feel this way, and it did not appear to me becoming to pursue your attentions further. I did not always keep to this resolve, finding myself on more than one occasion on the corner of your street watching outside your window for signs of suitors, or making cursory enquiries with your associates where you landed after Goldie sacked you.

You can imagine my happiness at learning that you are now the exclusive art representative of Thusnelda Baltuch. I can think of no one more deserving of this creditable position. I know there should be no reason for you to want any dealings with myself or Goldie, but I have been tasked by him personally to make whatever arrangements necessary to secure the best representations of Baltuch's work that you have available. There are no lengths that we will not go to acquire these pieces—no lengths. Goldie appreciates the history between the two of you, and has given me an impressive range from his collection with which to begin negotiations. A combination of selections from this grouping and cash value are also feasible (within reasonable limits). I cordially invite you to come to the gallery at your nearest convenience to discuss terms and selections, but know that Goldie would also be acquiescent to meeting at a more neutral location of your choosing. Please find enclosed some Stanisław Szukalski prints with Goldie's compliments. With apologies for the sprawling nature of this communication, and with sincerity and affection,

  –Serge

To MR. MAYACOU, of TORONTO

DEAR CUSTOMER,

Thank you for your interest in Thusnelda Baltuch's work. At this time, we are not making her pieces available publicly. We will notify you should this change. Regards,

  –T. Gotlieb-Ryder

MY MIND IS A BOGGLE-DE-BOTCH

To T.G.R., *of* TORONTO

TABITHA,

You can imagine Goldie's displeasure when the Baltuch pages went public without advance knowledge. The pieces he was interested in were no longer available by the time he had frantically approached one of your representatives at the opening reception of the Baltuch show. I would have been in for quite a hiding, I can assure you, had I not successfully moved a handful of Victor Moscoso pieces a few hours beforehand. Goldie was so blinded by rage that night that he hurled a bronze busk of his mother into the painting Marlana made in his likeness. The psychical implications of the act are, sadly, beyond me.

I saw you briefly by the Spitzweg painting—I did not know that you wore glasses. You looked radiant in crushed velvet, and your hair was very fetching in a chignon. Who was the gentleman who never left your side? Perhaps I overstep my bounds…

I have been authorized to offer two pieces as complimentary gifts, provided you and Baltuch agree to meet with Goldie at a location of your choosing: a Jack Cole *Betsy and Me* strip, which he recalls you admired on several occasions while in his employ, and a *Brenda Starr Reporter* strip by Ramona Fradon, which Baltuch has made no secret of admiring. I would never forgive myself if my neglectful behaviour in our relationship was somehow at the root of our inability to discuss business.

–S.

To T.G.R., *of* TORONTO

TABBY,

I am now hurriedly clearing the south wall of Goldie's lake home for the five Baltuch pieces he was able to secure from you at your La Castile meeting. Goldie and Marlana imparted to me in passing that some infelicitous things were mentioned at my expense (Marlana said she would elaborate when Goldie was asleep, but I can no longer tolerate being alone with that badger-legged woman after the sun has gone down. Bad enough she thinks we are married but not churched). I must admit that I find the experience of being brought so low at your hand extremely... stimulating. Your proviso that I must under no circumstances attend the meeting completed the enchantment. My mind is a boggle-de-botch; what must I do to obtain a response from you? After all, your will was my debasement (and can be again). Yours if you want it, a wife in watercolours, as it were,

   –Serge

BESPAWLER'S HANGING PLACE

To MR. MAYACOU, *of* TORONTO

BESPAWLER,

Cease all correspondence with me or face the consequences.
   –T. Gotlieb-Ryder

To SERGE MAYACOU, *of* TORONTO

SERGE,

I decided to break my silence after all these years because I heard the sad news of Goldie's passing. The community will undoubtedly be devastated. He was loud and brash, but he never laid a finger on me or treated me as anything less than an equal (except financially speaking of course). I had some fond memories while working for him, and our last meeting in the autumn to broker the Baltuch pieces was pleasant, painless. He spoke fondly of you at the dinner. He said you were like a son to him, and hoped you would take over the gallery after he retired and do your best not to run it into the ground. I suppose time has palliated my feelings of resentment for you to a degree. I appreciated you not writing me further after I insisted we break off communication. The world is a hanging place. Wishing you solace in this time of grieving,

–T. Gotlieb Ryder

To T.G.R., *of* TORONTO

TABBY,

Thank you for your thoughtful message. I confess I had lost all hope of ever communicating with you, in person or otherwise. It was a lovely gesture that cut me to the quick because of the nature of our romantic history. I often think about how our lives might have been different had I availed myself of a more courageous line of action at a critical juncture in our lives. Surely the position I now hold was not incommensurate with whatever potential we may have shared as lovers. I am filled with regret, but I realize the timing of a public disrobing of this nature is not entirely apropos.

The future of the gallery is uncertain. I want to continue on, but Marlana wants to unload the majority of the pieces to interested parties as soon as possible and sell the business; a few museums and private concerns have expressed interest in acquiring significant portions of Goldie's artwork en masse, sight unseen in some cases. If we entertain a liquidation, I would like to ensure the most deserving parties receive the most relevant pieces, which is to say, I do not want them collecting dust at a gallerist's warehouse because they are overpriced and deliberately out of reach, waiting for a Dominique de Menil to come nosing around like a truffle hog.

Marlana believes discrimination is unwarranted and wants to move to the south of France immediately. She wants us to be married at the moment it is (perceived) decent to do so. I am at cross purposes on that front, as it is compounding my stress over the funeral arrangements, of which I have (surprisingly) been charged with taking by the reins (where is Goldie and Marlana's daughter?!). I would be happy to return to you free of cost the Baltuch pieces—I understand Thusnelda has expressed regrets about letting those pieces go, and quite frankly, Marlana will not be aware of the minor financial loss. You are free to do with them as you wish; sell them again, keep them, et cetera. Think of it as a token of my everlasting appetency for what we shared, once upon a time.

—Serge

P.S. I further enclose the details of the funeral. You would be most welcome there, along with anyone you wish to bring.

To SERGE MAYACOU, *of* TORONTO

SERGE,

I just wanted to write to let you know that the ceremony was tastefully done and in accordance with every law of propriety. It is exactly the way Goldie would have wanted it, barring of course the spectacle Marlana made of herself. On no less than four occasions I saw her fondling your genitals in full view of Goldie's family. I can tell you that his mother especially did not care for the flagrant disrespect conferred on the dearly departed. I make no judgements as to who you share a bed with, but I would think that she could keep her hands to herself for a few blasted hours. Her behaviour was frankly indecorous and in shockingly bad taste.

I also want to ask about whose artwork hung above the casket. I have no recollection of the piece from the past, so assume it is a new work, perhaps one you commissioned on Goldie's behalf? It bore a passage about a "day at the beach" or a "blank ballot" if I am not misremembering. And if I dare skirt the edges of shamelessness myself, can I ask if it is for sale? I know you are in mourning and I would not be surprised at a less than propitious response (if any), but it has been some time since I have been moved to enquire about a piece for my ownership. Apologies in advance for the indiscretion,

   –Tabby

To T.G.R., *of* TORONTO

TABBY,

Apologies unnecessary. Your request was a happy intrusion into the sea of calamitous shit my life has become embroiled in. You are incorrect about the piece being from a new artist, but I cannot disclose at the moment whose hand was responsible. You will have to forgive this inflated need for secrecy, but the artist in question has asked that I not divulge their identity before they have completed the series to which it belongs. The pieces are rendered in a style considered a departure from their established credentials, and he has been wavering on the question of whether these shall ever be exhibited publicly or not. What I can tell you is that the inscription you have referred to is by Molavi, and reads as such:

X

Choosing the lesser evil
is choosing evil

Doing nothing is always an option
But what kind of nothing, my friend

A blank ballot
A day at the beach.

I thought it summed up Goldie's attitude toward political engagement rather well.

I will let the artist know that you have an interest in the work, and that you are also Baltuch's representative. Who knows? Perhaps I could have a good word with him about your talents for representation. Baltuch's profile has shot through the roof since she did those book-jacket designs for blewointment if I am not mistaken.

–Serge

HIGH FANTASTIC, HIGH DRUDGERY

To SERGE MAYACOU, *of* TORONTO

PRANNIE-MULCH,

You may have succeeded in lowering my defences, but you still have many flights up the campanile to run. Do not presume that because I now entertain your personal company that the errors and follies of the past can be erased like a candle snuffed out in a parlour room; neither must you comprehend my small allowances with greasing your gut-stick in my presence for a passport to every home port at my disposal. You have merely entered the barbican, and must consider yourself a stateless person. Your whore's bath this morning was the beginning of your variegated humiliations, trials and excoriations. I will make Giordano Bruno's sufferings look like a morning constitutional compared to what you will endure at my hands. You will *not* be moving to Lourmarin, and you will *not* be selling off Goldie's gallery. I will direct your every movement and stratagem with regard to Marlana. Am I understood, Manfat? We will engineer the swift dissolution of whatever fishmongering commerce you were caught up in with Madame Pudge—no need to die on that hill. My list of demands shall be forthcoming. Scorf up the medicine now, little sissified itch-mite. Remember, this isn't high fantastic after all, this is high drudgery. The Glitz Cunt is dead. Long live the Glitz Cunt.

–T.G.R.

P.S. Press this letter to your nose and relive the fragrance of my putrescence. I had to see a star about a twinkle.

To SERGE MAYACOU, *of* TORONTO

GASH-HOUND,

Hilt and hair time will be further delayed. What follows is a list of my counter-value targets. Stand by for concurrence, leather stretching to follow.

1. You will surrender all mid- to high-grade art in your possession to me at no later time than a week from receipt of this annexing letter. Supplemental to this requirement are all paper records and inventories pertaining to said collection.

2. The forfeiture of these assets must occur on the lawn of Quail Pipe Manor, my place of residence, at the stroke of midnight on the night of the next blood moon (next Tuesday), wearing only a smile and after quaffing a vial of quebrachine, which I shall provide in preposterous quantities.

3. For each article of art surrendered, you shall perform a short ritual of my devising, which I shall elucidate in detail. The ritual, hereinafter referred to as the SHUSH BAG, consists in the nibble and dribble of the scads of diamond-shaped bum oodles that are currently plaguing my nethers while you keep the census down. After each vitiation of seed, you will be allowed a short respite for hydration (quebrachine or water only). No gel packs will be provided.

4. After this game of pebble dashing is concluded, you will undoubtedly need ample time for recovery. You will avail yourself of the amenities of Quail Pipe for no less than twenty-four hours, both to familiarize yourself in your new environs and become acquainted in the barracks with the other Sweetcorn Boys. There will be no quarter on this account. There will be no room for Marlana this night.

5. When sufficient mindfulness has returned to your faculties, you will convene in the sub-level man-pits for locally televised shew-combat. Report to Claude and Aldegonde for sanitation and oiling. Clinch holds are strongly encouraged.

6. Your future with me as Head Buggerclaw will depend entirely on this contest of wretches. I will not be undone by your pusillanimity again. Fight for your keepsakes as much as you fight for your Great Winnower. When and only when you have surpassed these requirements will my demands continue.

Assholes in retrograde,
   –The Great Winnower

To SERGE MAYACOU, *of* TORONTO

GLEETBAG,

Your inventory is in shambles! I will have you consume more Stramonium and Bynin Amara if you cannot be brought to heel. I know from memory that you had in your possession Martin Van Maële, Ed Valigursky and Paul Lehr originals. I also distinctly recall a Frank Wilson drawing from *Supermanship* ("The Great Vice Versa"). Obfuscate again and the night physicals shall be accompanied with a very cold Roboleine spoon.

–Tabs *qua* Tabs

QUAIL PIPE DRIPPYDICK'S ALL DUFF AND NO GROG

To T.G.R., *of* TORONTO

GATEKEEPER OF TABBYDOM,

Happy tidings on the Marlana question. She has taken my disappearance rather poorly I am told; her crying fits have spilled out into public spaces now. Rumours abound that she cannot continue on without me, and has splendidly made one attempt already at taking her own life involving a piece of chicken wire (I shall spare you the details). The police have been notified concerning my disappearance, and I reckon they shall approach you about an interview for questioning. I feel my resolve failing, which is not to say that I do not believe in the "saturnalias of our conventicle" as you term it, but then again, a rubber truncheon in less capable hands makes for less desirable results.

I don't want to let you down again. I realize that breaking off communication was what doomed us the first time, so instead I want to make my fears perfectly understandable and ask for assurances (come what may). As irresistible as the attractions of Quail Pipe are, I am beginning to bristle at being under the floorboards for so long (there are only so many Hy Averback films you can watch). Couldn't I step out to pick up a few things, Dovey? I might have to run an errand in Moss Park for a night or two…

I really think you are taking too much on your shoulders. Claude is a dear, but the polybabble that passes for conversation is so astonishingly poor that I really might quash his quongs one night with a coat hanger—I am sure that you would grant me that much. What a radgepot you have running this madhouse; châteaued out of his mind half the time from jimmyjohns he's hoisted out the cellar and rolled into his quarters.

In more cheerful news, I received word through protected channels from an old friend. Ingram Freleng, upon hearing of my disappearance after Goldie's death, began to fear for the worst. Far from presuming that I was absconding from the scene of a crime, his letter of concern went to great lengths to assure me that I had a friend who wanted to repay an old debt. He seems enthusiastic about paying homage to Goldie's legacy, and has expressed an interest in fencing the majority of the collection to international parties at white-market pricing. We will not be sending more than two pieces per party (and none to France, naturally) to ensure they are not consolidated in one pool, and trackable by the authorities. But perhaps we should make some small allocation for Marlana—she will after all have limited means in Europe, and I do feel she will be hard done by, even *if* we make arrangements on her behalf.

Eagerly awaiting your return from the west. I have not moused off during your absence, as promised. I hope you will be feeling better in a few days. I agree with your sentiment that summer colds are the worst: predictably ill-timed, with a hint of insouciance for good measure. My anxiety unseats my mind. I fear it has made me disastrously unproficient in the goodly art of letter-writing. Adieu for now, your

–Serge

To SERGE MAYACOU, of TORONTO

DRIPPYDICK, LOVETICK, STYPDICK,

You Cooper Union dropouts are all the same. All duff and no grog, ineluctably doomed by a lack of imagination. I left Bella Coola earlier than communicated and should be arriving shortly after this letter reaches you. DO NOT SET FOOT OUTSIDE OF QUAIL PIPE YOU DERMOPHILIAC DUCK SHIT UNLESS YOU WANT ABROGATIONS OF YOUR PRIVILEGES TO RESULT. You will receive an Arthur Ranson if you comply.

Your recalcitrance will be our undoing. Claude has already apprised me of your undisciplined self-gratifications. Evirates are my speciality, remember?

Claude has rummaged through your rubbish and found enough evidence to damn an onery house. A night-diddle to buy his silence counts for hardly anything in today's delicate economy. I run a tight ship, Jagabat. Never forget where you are—sowgelders aplenty.

Marlana is no longer a concern. I went to Bella Coola in part to negate her involvement in our future. Her kitling Prue Enz lives there, remember? We have always been on good terms. Goldie had long suspected that Prue was not produced of his bloodline.

I have to impart the paramount importance of my next question: you are *absolutely certain* Goldie included an infidelity or non-paternity event clause in his prenuptial agreement? I don't need to know particulars. I am with Prue as I write this, who assures me there is no love lost between her and her mother. Her recollection is that Goldie pledged to her that in the final event, she would be taken care of, but that should any proofs of Marlana's inconstancy turn up, Prue could expect courtly munificence on his part. Prue had always construed that to mean she would receive the Stanley Pitt painting. Whether or not this in actuality means, as I suspect, the whole kit and caboodle of the inheritance, you are my proof for this legal eventuality taking place and leaving Marlana to toy with only otiose recriminations in solitude and wonder.

I will give Marlana the option of giving chase to her *roi fainéant* and losing all stately entitlements to Prudence, or that of keeping the villa in Lourmarin, along with her share of the bequeathment (minus the unaccounted-for artworks), and the abandonment of her search of one "missing" business partner. Another fly jockey wants looking after. What else is new? Is that a happy enough ending for you or do you want to go again?

More gambitfields to follow.

–Tabs

Baie-du-Tombeau (Dire Moi Ene Coup Ki Qualite Couillon Sa)

SEGA-BOOGIE

Aka aka boule caca
Lever mayonet ista tac
Aka aka boule caca .
Lever mayonet ista tac
Aka aka boule caca
Lever mayonet ista tac
Aka aka boule caca
Lever mayonet ista tac

Quelle domage!
Inne tombe someil
Inne gaspiaze nous les temps
Cot to croire inne
Fine trouve sa larriage la?

REFRAIN
Attend ene ti malin (quoi?)
Cot la riviere
Zoine di vent...
Di vent...
Di vent...
Zoine di vent...
Di vent...
Di vent...

Aka aka boule caca
Lever mayonet ista tac
Aka aka boule caca
Lever mayonet ista tac
Aka aka boule caca
Lever mayonet ista tac
Aka aka boule caca
Lever mayonet ista tac

What a pity!
He nodded off
Squandering all our time
Where do you think he
Found this jackanapes?

REFRAIN
Wait for a malapert (what?)
Where the river
Joins the wind...
The wind...
The wind...
Joins the wind...
The wind...
The wind...

149

Attend en ti malin (quoi?)	Wait for a malapert (what?)
Dire moi ene coup	Tell me one thing
Ki quali...	What kind...
Quali...	Kind...
Quali...	Kind...
Ki quali...	What kind...
Quali...	Kind...
Quali...	Kind...
Ki qualite couillon?	What kind of sod is this?
Li pu gate so les doigts	He's gonna spoil his fingers
Li pu gate so li nez	He's gonna spoil his nose
Alle rode ki part	Look around
Pu to sulazman	For a jolt of skag
Grate to fesse	Itch your ass
Couma ene vaurien	Like a sluggard
Faire galant colonne lor barrier	Skirt-chasing by the fence
Baise to chemin!	Out of my sight!
Allez!	Go on!

REFRAIN   **REFRAIN**

All Songs by Kaartikeya Derwish (Mauritian Countryside Plenitude Publishing Company)

As to Birdlime

DISUTILITY AND ITS APPOINTMENTS

Far more injurious to the organization of a society, and posing
more threat of abandonment in their actions than able imagin-
ations can supply, are not the downtrodden outcasts but are
erupted out of the selfsame fabric, subsequently charged with
its undermining and whose numbers are comparatively insignificant: the innumerable personages comprising a generation
of groutheads bleeding out the world through their disutility,
excuse-making and recreant idleness deserve this honour in
the gross. Taken in total, the detriment of such actions produce
more turmoil and languor than any single act of mortal violence; for disutility in its own right is a common enough trait
in humanity, haphazard though it may be in its appointments;
but given time, such inclinations harden into habit and further
consolidate into vice, where it is in an estimable position to produce disquietude on a level unparalleled in this bye-corner of
the world, even considering the many horrors of the blade, the
pistol and of the gnarled neck, evidenced in the case of Claude
Ste. Croix, the man of a hundred epithets who forsooth shocked
unsparing men unto wild paroxysms averring to his lame and
prodigious uselessness.

Leaving behind a young mother with child, Ste. Croix trav-
elled to the Home District to seek his fortune; to ply his abilities

in a situation where his standing might not fail him gainful opportunities. He felt wondrously justified in his action, for that he reasoned he would be better suited in a pecuniary sense to support his stripling; even if such support came at the cost of being unable to witness the progress of his little Aldegonde by his own account, at the very least—he would console himself when thoughts occasioned on the subject of his conscience— his child would not grow hungry or unhoused; draped in rags to be sure, but woe betide he who had neither the fortune nor the good sense to view it as a blessing, draped in *something* nevertheless.

THE ANTERIOR FINISHED STATE

The amelioration of one's circumstances does not always invigorate a winnowed spirit, however; nor does it bolster one's efforts against the toing and froing of destiny; for any wight can fall more steadily into depravity and lose heart against debilities which are ever gnawing at the back of a troubled mind when the simple comforts afforded one's station are well stocked and matched with the allure of unfamiliarity.

How absolute the decline from anterior experiences that work one's demeanour into a finished state is entirely a question of what influences went into concerting it, for aught I know, and it does not take long for observers in Ste. Croix's company to realize that his character champs at two opposing impulses that work over his mind like the dastardly elements the heavens above and barathrum below: an envy over fallal, gewgaw and other symbols of pride what reigns with unchecked purpose in his worm-ridden breast, simultaneously held fast by a failure to acknowledge the requisite means to attain these profligate objectives, resulting in his choleric attachment to violence. But one cannot begrudge a man a crown befitting his station when the results of this mental impasse are so manifold.

Alone in an unacquainted land, he desires acceptance and takes to the pretensions of the faddist with great avidity. He covers his shoulders with the finest accoutrements, sometimes rationalizing that ostentation will lead to further independence and recognition. Setting upon and then boring of the use of hackney-coaches and gigs, the consumption of alarming volumes of libations and the effecting of nocturnal conquests at the bawdy-house, his preferences soon begin to veer away from boyhood pleasures (though one could argue withal the opposite) and instead are marshalled to the necessitous tune of anyone who will oblige a word to his bending ear, seeking to push this new, rather exploitable acquaintance along the way to (mutual, it must needs be said) advancement.

A TRADEMAN'S ART

Ste. Croix's possessions ranged from the dull to the profane, and he ensured a good many hours were wasted on allowing his intellectual prowess—never one to shine too brightly—fall further into destitution. There were many months where he put aside his obligations just past Bytown in favour of forgetting them outright, and in so doing, began to render absent the memory of owing any such connexion of responsibility (his many crapulous conquests which he would wend his way with interlocked arms down the road from a public house to his rusticated dwelling, attested firmly to this conviction).

But so formidable and attractive were Ste. Croix's hidden talents that he enticed a coterie of distinguished men from all quarters of the city with his services at a quick moment's dispatch, the exact nature of which shall forthwith be related in our history. His abilities soon recommended him to the attention of those who could procure his advancement in genteel circles; his company amongst these scoundrels required him to gain a stronger proficiency in his second language (none to which such an ambition could fault), to recite their gentlemanly norms toward the fairer sex, to pay these drawlatches for their stalwart mentorship and to save enough capital to follow his true calling in life: to serve the community in the capacity of a respected carpenter.

When he was not employed at a sponging house, he spent many hours blazing a trail of wood particles into the air, sending the fragrant aromas of finely hewn birch through the corridors of his cheapjack domicile, let those who would witness such arrogance find succour where they could (the end of a bottle usually). Ste. Croix would animatedly convey his aspirations to any who would hear him, citing his lack of mastery over the language as his chief hindrance to an apprenticeship; and often within the same breath, he would declare his abundant orders for dropleaf tables, chaises and Chippendale cabinets from stately gentlefolk, though he would suffer no one to see his finished works with the exception of paying customers. Howsoever his allowances for pleasure constrained his pocket, it was certain that an ever-greater part of his wages were devoted to lightening the ailments of his tedium: if he could not exhaust the pent-up anxieties of a day's toiling labour warding the dagger hands of indigent debtors, surely he would not be fit to carry the same enthusiasm the following day, let alone its continuation in perpetuity, along with his dedication to a tradesman's art.

SILVER IN A RAKEHELL'S PURSE

Ste. Croix had an aptitude for self-delusion and many ventured it his greatest of personal weaknesses. Perhaps hearkening back to his beggarly childhood, he knew the value of *pathos* and was delivered of it extremely well: "I have too much on my mind, your pulchritude, to take stock of when the week's waste must be deposited," he would mutter like a whipped dog to his neighbours, the oversight of his duties to adequately hinder the overflowing of waste in the back lanes of his lodgings being the subject of disputation; for Ste. Croix was very well delivered of his mother's admonitions, who advised that he who had not silver in his purse, must have it on his tongue.

There is a species of wretchedness exemplified by people in whose company enjoyment and commiseration may be had, though they be generally undependable and wayward in their attentions. Such was the place reserved for Ste. Croix's specific brand of companionship, which in many ways serves as the poorest, most fatuous of human relations. Better a man you can know with certainty to be a rogue that will pocket your money at his first opportunity and wherein you avoid for monumental favours, than a tonsured abomination who wears the flesh of a man but conceals the unrepentant stirrings of a rakehell. The inveteracy of his forgetfulness evoked such indignation from his fellows that they fell to leaving reminders of his duties, though it worked no effect on his movements. It seemed that nothing could rouse the oaf to accept even this modest claim to society.

NATURE'S SUPREMITY

There was, strangely enough, one responsibility to which Ste. Croix felt committed, and which was truthfully so binding as to controul his every movement in the birdlime of onerous remembrance. One of Ste. Croix's consorts left in his charge a Manks kitten upon the severance of their romantic dally. The reasons for his acceptance of the importunity, when he had proven so tenderfooted in his efforts for the sake of others, is alas, subject only to our readers' best conjecture. But for the testament to the relationship's longevity, mayhap it could be surmised that the upkeep of the imperial animal would have been forsook entirely?

To witness the calumnies this noble creature was forced to receive at his master's hands would usher godly ordinances for a slow demise at the gallows; only the lowest of wretches, the forfeiture of justice being a natural conclusion of their villainy, could inflict such horrors on a featureless animal, which in the case of this much-maligned prisoner, lived in a space no bigger than a bolt hole, and whose accommodations were in such a state of ruination as to suggest habitual and perfected neglect. Frequently by way of punishment, the Manks was shorn of its majestic coat; divots mottled its hide when tufts were coldly removed with a bone knife, its many wounds delivered of an unsteady, intoxicated hand. Sirrah! How such a knave could outlive this model of Nature's supremacy, the work of her delicate and masterful hand, afflicts the beatings of a now-stilled heart!

A RASCALLY PREFERENCE

When he could eschew his commitments no more, which is to say, when he could no longer equivocate in his letters the subject of his avoidance, lest he be branded with the baseborn stain of illegitimacy, he made arrangements for a return to Beauharnois to see how his Aldegonde was faring, and to reside in a place where he did not have to expend the energy required to keep his belly lined, for that he expected a feast befitting a royal welcome; and where is there surer guarantee of being waited on with sedulity than in the company of one's own materfamilias?

He made no secret of his ungovernable satisfaction to his neighbours, and he thought on the happy excursions he would make with his new flame, Agatha, a stout-armed hoyden whose countenance immoderately suggested the image of certain low-lying, heavy-pelaged mammalia whom only the vulgar would dare mention in pages such as these. Ste. Croix did not notify his estranged wife of these late developments, and instead pulled her aside upon his arrival to discuss a confederation of attentions with Agatha the Large. Upon his wife's refusal, however, he resolved that he no longer had use for her comely attentions. The news was not received well by the young mother, who flew into such a warranted rage, and held back nothing of the censorious emotion that seized her organ of amativeness, that Claude was repelled into a corner with such force and rapidity as to knock down a beauteous arrangement of dishes and a framed portrait of his own mother, which was, in the roving movements that followed the outburst, torn asunder beyond hope of repair.

Marcelline, such was the jilted woman's name, had wrenched the philanderer's collar into such a fantastic mash of flesh that verily did his eyes begin to slide out of their watering sockets, as did his countenance take on such an unhealthy arrangement that G-d wot the entire family—assembled for the welcoming celebration—was all that stood in the way of an untimely addition to the growing and already-substantial family plot. Once she was no longer all aflutter, Marcelline gave such a moving address as to shock the brute into awareness of the baneful slight he had conducted against her, the charges of which included caitiff prevarications and cruel remissness. She concluded her tirade with such an enumerated list of his various shortcomings as a disabled participant in the arts of sensuality that a roar of mirthful gaiety broke out amongst the homestead that could be heard well into the adjacent apartment.

When the flaring of tempers had subsided, all were composed enough to be arranged at the table. The parties in attendance solicited the tales of excitation that preceded Claude and Agatha's arrival; this in turn, out of politeness, was followed by enquiries as to their first meeting. Marcelline could not help glaring at the woman who had lately occupied her abdicated position; who had succeeded in capturing Claude's rascally preference. The remainder of the night moved for her at an awkward pace, a slightly over-treated roast, the many antiscorbutic entrees and a well-lined belly, all which stood in the way of her dependable revenge.

Agatha, who spoke not a word of French and held company with individuals who did not understand G-d's English, was left muddled on the horns of a dilemma. She grew annoyed with her lover, who made no visible effort of translation. Great was her surprise when she became acquainted with the fact that Claude had concealed the existence of a daughter. She minced not her words that night in the privacy of their bedroom, announcing that she would not halve her resources for a child that meant nothing to her, and that she would not take pains for any soul other than on the behalf of her own flesh and blood.

ALDEGONDE

The impact that the visit made on Aldegonde in the course of the next few days did not go unnoticed by the Ste. Croix family. Claude seemed more taken with the idea of visiting old companions he had not seen and who, more importantly, could stand him a drink to celebrate his return—which was all the more reason for him to make such rencounters to their homes individually. Aldegonde could always sense the bitterness with which her mother was accustomed to speaking about her father, but having no recollection of the man, elected to suspend her judgement until she could decide for herself exactly what kind of character he bore. There were not enough of these so-called qualities for her to register feelings as complicated as hate, but a plenitude of convictions soon passed sentence on the man and disowned him of a paternal relation, out of apathy if for no other reason.

EBULLITIONS OF TERROR

There is one final event during his travels that it credits us to
convey, and it concerns the reasons Claude was forced to beat a
hasty retreat back to Upper Canada. A month into his holiday,
he was bouncing his stripling on his lap, attempting to inveigle
responses to his coddling, when he suddenly became white as
a ghost, as if struck with a glancing blow to the head. To the
noticeable change in his mien, Aldegonde was affected enough
to enquire as to his apparently failing health; but Claude could
not avert his eyes from the scene that played out in the dusty
street before him. Two animals were competing over a fetching
scrap of meat, the hardier of the two being a sour-faced Manks
who clawed wildly with ebullitions of terror. In his reverie,
Claude stood up with great discomposure, letting his child fall
into a bramble, and made his way to the house to arrange for
his immediate departure. He informed his mother of the supposed calenture to which Agatha had surrendered, having been
unaccustomed to the inclement weather, and wished the age-
ing, withered woman the best for the future until the time of
her passing.

Agatha, who had been newly acquainted with the unknown
pleasures of horse-riding, and at the time of his calling engaged
in a hearty jaunt, fell to darker moods yet again, and unleashed
lusty rejoinder after another during their abrupt packing,
hasty farewells (though none that included little Aldegonde,
who could not be found at the time) and finally their arrival
at Garrison Creek. She was not made to understand the need
for diligence, though she made numerous expatiations to her
lover's need to apprise her of the reasons of the many travelling

expenditures they were forced to suddenly make, all apparently in the service of some great caprice.

THE FOUR STAGES OF CRUELTY

All through the thunder of her tireless pleas, Claude was silent, until he disembarked with his luggage from his rented brougham and put his key into the lock of his apartment. Crossing the threshold, a mischief of mice flew out between his legs, and dispelling all the suspicions that turned in her mind, Agatha saw the signs of starvation firmly impressed upon the Manks' enfeebled frame, the swollen head rendering it the quality of a rag doll, and its prickly coat reminiscent of flotsam drying on the surf while covered in tangles of ocean weeds. She recoiled from horror and began to wretch into the garden bed while Claude marvelled at the stupidity of his handiwork.

With unprecedented haste, Claude made for a trowel that had been embedded deep within the dead soil with the intention of implementing the removal of the body to a far less conspicuous situation where it would not likely attract the attention of unwanted, but more importantly, retaliatory witnesses who could make a report to the landowner who held the Four Stages of Cruelty to such an exemplary regard, that only a confirmed lover of animals could hold the position of groundskeeper. But as man, woman and Devil are the only three degrees of comparison, Ste. Croix's mind very naturally turned to thoughts of his deliverance, and what his mistress with whom he shared custody of the animal would say. His mind was so labyrinthine with doubt that he cleft the body with as many accidental incisions as to form a passageway for the decomposing organs to pour out. Never let it be said that Claude did not possess some strange intrepidity that, though it would never serve his desires in the way of fortune, providence or happiness, could make bold affronts against impending dangers that threatened.

VIL CUR

Emptying a Hessian sack that contained his clothes, he laid out the carcass delicately on the fulcrum of his trowel and let the animal fall to the bottom, realizing at the last moment that some of Agatha's linens had accumulated at the base, wedged down by moisture and compression. Sensing her approach, he fastened the sack and ran past her, wedging her in the threshold in the process, before finally wrestling free and delivering one final trepan against her.

"Do not concern your head my dearest, for I will dispose of this nuisance with expediency to rival that of the Devil himself!" he called out feverishly before disappearing through a gathering fog. Hitting upon a plan to satisfy himself of an escape, he bound together the loose articles of refuse that had accumulated in his absence, and combined it with the carcass so that he could make away betimes and return before any of his neighbours could impute the stercoraceous bouquet of putrefaction that presided athwart the air to any other cause.

Upon his return, Ste. Croix was resolved to compose a letter that would tie off his last loose end in this disaster, *viz.* a cessation of relations with the mistress with whom he shared ownership of the Manks he had just condemned to the depths of Garrison Creek, and who on occasion, when she desired to savour in the pleasures of a coital embrace by a furtive assignation, made pretence to enquire as to the health of her cherished and much-beloved animal. He was prevented from actuating this plan, however, when on returning, he found a letter already addressed to him from Agatha the Large, who had taken what remained of her things and left for sunnier prospects. The letter read as follows: *Yor faylures as a luver ar owtdon ownly by yor faylures as a man. You ar not fit to crowl the surfase of this urth you wiked, vil cur.*

SUPERANNUATIONS OF HOPE

Expecting the best outcome, and to that effect denoting the foolishness of not putting stock in superannuations of hope, the inhabitants of Ste. Croix's abode rejoiced to see their back lanes finally cleared, and briefly entertained the expectation that Claude had been animadverted on his oversights by the landowner. They were rewarded instead for this impractical optimism with a mystery concerning the one and only instance wherefore this feckless groundskeeper was inspired both by the urgency of precipitous movements and tight-lipped secrecy to execute an honourless charge.

The Lost Norman: A Preview

PARALLEL STYLE OF PROVOCATION

> *"Often consideration of a poor example, by virtue of its imperfection, tells one more than consideration of a prime example, in its perfection."*

–Patrick Hughes and George Brecht

Modwind is tilling the field with several other space-labourers. The artificial sun is blisteringly hot. Effulgent waves warp and glaze over a desolate, rayless, alien reality. Modwind vainly attempts to wipe his brow from under an oversized desert campaign cap with a sun flap curiously placed over a bubble helmet. An antenna protrudes slightly through the cap, though it does not puncture it. Modwind has somehow snuck off a piece of fruit from one of the shrubs he is tending; he is enjoying the refreshment it provides from inside his helmet, unable to manoeuvre the food except with his chin, teeth and lip against the inside of the fishbowl.

He is staring off into the distance when domesticated mutant thrumwort plants cross his line of sight; his eyes soon come alive with stupefaction—the sight stands revealed. One of the thrumworts has swelled to colossal proportions, has perambulated deep into the penned-in enclosure where the labourers work. It kicks aside a now empty bag labelled GROWTH FEED—USE IN

MODERATION. The plant has mutated into a monstrosity: twelve feet high, more ungainly than usual and towering over everything in its path. Its encumbered movements sway toward the workers, its leaf-feet weighted down with iridium. Modwind is stabbing the air with his garden hoe, screaming muted whelps through a radio-fuzzed walkie. He makes scalping movements at the vegetative predator. *Shwank, shwank* in stereo.

His colleagues have wisely evacuated the pen and stand huddled inside a cockpitless hovercraft, quaking with fear and motioning their friend over. Modwind is the only one left to save the yield. The thrumwort picks up Modwind by the legs and turns him upside down. Modwind is shaking wildly, but somehow still manages to grip the hoe; he slashes at the amaranth's bosom of fruit bulbs. It lets loose a waterphone keening into the zero-grav heavens. One must take precautions against isolation-bred space-cafard any way they can, even in thankless risk-taking (most of the yield does not make it to Earth intact anyway). Modwind falls to the soil in slow motion, the background behind him exploding into fractals of light. Title in relief, spinning out from Modwind's heart, and growing larger and larger: *The Fat of the Land.*

Modwind's flailing torso blurs into a water rippling effect, giving way to the very picture of domestic placidity—a tiny, non-futuristic kitchen where Modwind, free of his tubular-ringed gyro-suit, sat leisurely at his dinner table, is scooping leaves of lettuce reminiscent of the caudatus leaf into an outsized autolyzed yeast spread jar in the same fashion as Space-Gardener's hoe-parrying. Modwind happily sheens his teeth with the lettuce strips as one would masticate leaves of tobacco, the sounds of his contented smacking occasionally interrupted by intense, guttural inarticulations from the recesses of his throat. The wireless by the kitchen counter, which had moments ago been playing a song in the same key as the waterphone wails from the opening scene, suddenly rasps to life.

"We interrupt this regularly scheduled broadcast for a special bulletin. Breaking news from the Cuthbertson estate in North Warwickshire: A.D. Cuthbertson, president and founder of Cuthbertson Industries, has died of natural causes. He passed away in his private residence surrounded by a small circle of business confidants and legal representatives. An announcement from a Cuthbertson Industries representative is forthcoming. It is believed that Mr. Cuthbertson had no heirs to his sizeable, property-based fortune. More on this story as it develops."

Modwind had slowly risen in increments upon hearing each sense-shattering particular of the bulletin, his cranking teeth stalling and then drawing to a close mid-mouthful. The camera tracks in tightly on his face where the whites of his eyes register aspiration and disbelief. No sooner do the dulcet melodies of a swing number erupt from the wireless than Modwind is out the door of his apartment, racing down a flight of seemingly endless stairs. He emerges from the cramped interior of his apartment into a bustling market square. Modwind crosses frenetically through the bevy of extras but he is being swallowed whole by the tide of people, his bobbing head the only indication that he still exists within this crush of swirling bodies. His trademark bandit cap with its flared visor is occasionally almost knocked over, but by some sort of filmic resolve, it remains anchored to its topgallant. Modwind vainly pipes up with a few "Well, I nevers," and "My words." Reaching the other side of the street— after shaking his fists and kicking the air near the assembly line of marching feet—Modwind knocks at the first door he has come to.

"Wake up, Mr. Smidlarge, wake up!" he howls. "It's happened, Mr. Smidlarge, the day we've been waiting for!"

A Brilliantined head covered in shaving cream pops out of the second-storey window and the uncharacteristically unspectacled visage of Mr. Smidlarge squints incision-sized suspicion at Modwind.

"What is it now, Oscar? You're liable to wake the dead with all that hollering."

"Mr. Smidlarge, Old Man Cuthbertson has died! I've just heard it on the morning news!"

"Well, why didn't you say so? Come on up, then, but don't wake Clara or I'll be up to my ears in trouble. Not the foyer. Go through the back, Oscar, the back!"

With atomically-propulsed glee, Modwind runs around the Smidlarge residence and shimmies up a downpipe, wherefrom he leaps onto a garden trellis. The trellis, however, is unbalanced, and begins to sway side-to-side with the weight of Modwind's body. The scene cuts to Clara in her nightie powdering her face in the bathroom. At the sight of Modwind's mooning face in her mirror, Clara disregards the impression as a figment of her imagination. With each passing interval of Modwind's head, a slide whistle dips up and down. By the third or fourth pass, Clara has turned around. The scene shifts to Mr. Smidlarge shaving in his washroom. A feminine scream shatters the peace and an ear-splitting crash sends the frame of the film rocking, nudging Smidlarge's arm so that he cuts himself shaving.

A fade slowly brings into view the stationary bodies of Modwind, a chin-bandaged Mr. Smidlarge and his wife Clara seated around the breakfast table. Modwind is a bustle of energy trying to contain itself.

"Well, go on and tell her, Mr. Smidlarge! That you stand to inherit it all!"

"Inherit what, darling?" Clara chimes.

Mr. Smidlarge gives a strained look of disapproval to Oscar, his eyes looking out from over his glasses.

"It's like this, love. A.D. Cuthbertson, the richest man in our fair town, has died, but his estate and assets are subject to escheat. However, me own mother brought me up with the notion that I was the sole by-product of their, er, unwearying romance. She had evidence to support this, of which I am in possession."

"Oh my! Well, isn't that exciting!"

"Today I shall put my case forward with the managers of my estranged father's estate, and we shall have restitution for my life in the repellant shadows."

Clara's eyes momentarily look away from her cup of tea as the word "repellant" is uttered.

"Do you think you shall be well received?"

"Of course he'll be well received, Clara. Mr. Smidlarge is, after all, Mr. Cuthbertson's own flesh and blood."

"Me own father denied every communication I sent him. Just because we have the truth on our side does not mean we've won the day. It's only natural that there will be some infighting regarding my, some will say, all-too-timely arrival."

"But there's nothing timely about it, Mr. Smidlarge. If anything, you were too late to save him!"

The scene shifts to the closest thing to a sky-scraping, matte-enhanced corporate building the small town has on offer. It is noticeably out of place among the scrabble of modest, worn-down buildings of Merseylinton—its roof is not even visible. The Cuthbertson logo is engraved on a two-ton stone megalith that welcomes visitors by the *porte-cochère* looming over the entrance doors. The camera pans upward rapidly until the windows blur into a shiver of lights before stopping and craning in on the executive suite at the top of the building. Four executives in boxy, bespoke suits are debating the future of Cuthbertson Industries.

"That's where you're wrong, Tunleyh," a dyspeptic, starched-shirt type named Mr. Emedonds cautions. "The Cuthbertson future *is* in danger. Just you wait and see what we shall have crawling out the woodwork."

"No need for hysterics," Mr. Tunleyh rejoins. "Measures have been put in place to maintain a sense of stability. Bring in Ailsa, please. Gentlemen of the board, allow me to introduce to you the rightful successor of the great Cuthbertson name."

Through a panelled door, a charmless woman enters the boardroom in a chequered-print dress with her eyes held firmly on the tips of her shoes. She stops at the foot of the hardwood conference table.

"Ailsa Cuthbertson."

A commotion erupts from the three other executives.

"Piffle!"

"Oh botheration! He's actually done it!"

"Gentlemen, gentlemen! Allow me a moment to explain. Allan indeed produced no biological heirs. Ailsa is a young woman he took on as his ward in secrecy. He has been financing her studies and vocational training in an arrayed field of economics and business for years now, has shaped her mind in the mould of his own."

"How do we know this isn't some ploy to undermine the rest of us?"

A montage of young Ailsa playing in the street commences while a sound bridge of Tunleyh's exposition plays over.

"You have before you now Ailsa's adoption papers. Allan saw this gamine on the streets wherever he went. Property development sites, the country club…"

A ball rolls into the street and a shoeless child shown from the knees down darts after it. A black car comes into frame before screeching to a stop. The sound of a car door opening is followed by a close-up of an adult hand holding out the ball. The boardroom comes into view again. An executive's hand is holding a wad of scrunched tobacco in a graphic match of the preceding scene. The tobacco is adroitly stuffed into a pipe.

"Moved by her depths of hardship, he took her to breakfast one morning," Tunleyh continues. "She demonstrated an inborn facility with numbers."

"Shame we couldn't say the same about Allan," the pipe-smoking executive mutters to Edemonds.

"Regarding Allan's relative secrecy in the matter, I think your attitudes speak for themselves."

"Tunleyh, you can't expect us to go along with this. To reserve a seat on the board for a woman we know nothing about?"

"We must honour Allan's final wishes. He asked that we allow her a period of time to prove herself. Time alone will tell whether she will earn a place beside us in the administration of this board."

A crossfade soon reveals Mr. Smidlarge and Oscar tramping their way up to Cuthbertson HQ accompanied by a tuba sonatine. They approach the reception desk and are ignored by the carefree, prim-looking receptionist.

"Ahem."

The receptionist makes no gesture of recognition.

"Hello, dear. A Mr. Smidlarge and Mr. Modwind to see a Cuthbertson representative."

"Do you have an appointment?" the receptionist drawls with characteristically anodyne low feeling.

"No, as a matter of fact, we don't," Oscar chirrups.

"I really can't let you—"

"Now wait a minute, ma'am, wait a minute. Please understand. My name is Mr. Smidlarge. It's regarding a *sensitive* personal matter of some *grave* importance."

"Oh, let me guess. This is about the Cuthbertson estate? Heredity and Filiation."

"I beg your pardon, madam?"

"You'll be wanting to join the queue. Up the stairs and to the right."

"But I've—"

"Heredity and Filiation. Up the stairs and to the right."

Mr. Smidlarge and Oscar scale the stairs. They emerge on the second floor and collectively wince at the sight of hundreds of people lining up under an ad hoc sign scrawled in fresh paint that reads *Heredity and Filiation.* Ailsa Cuthbertson is standing conspicuously behind the administrative nodes at the end of the hallway processing the army of heir apparents born practically overnight.

"I think we're out of luck, Mr. Smidlarge."

"Except that we have the truth on our side, lad. Never forget that. Move along then, Oscar. We'll lose our precedence."

Through the miracle economy of the time-lapse, Smidlarge and Modwind come to the reception desk. Ailsa has taken particular notice of this curious duo before her.

"Hullo, my name is Smidlarge. Rewdilf Smidlarge."

"I suppose you're brothers?" an H&F functionary remarks sarcastically.

"What? Oh no, this is my colleague, Mr. Modwind. I don't know about the rest of these impostors, but I am the true son of the late Allan Cuthbertson."

"And you have documentation supporting this allegation?"

"I do, making it no mere allegation. A birth certificate, notarized by my mother and Mr. Cuthbertson's assistant Mr. Emedonds, records of a trust in my name disbursed annually, and letters my father wrote to my mother."

The functionary swallows a hard lump of humility before Ailsa interjects.

"Good morning. Please allow me to introduce myself. I am the superintending officer of the Heredity and Filiation Department. Who did you say your mother was?"

"Emas Smidlarge. But don't you think this is a subject better discussed in private, madam?"

"Yes, of course, Mr. Smidlarge. Please follow me."

Ailsa, Oscar and Smidlarge enter single file into a cramped corner office, but before the door can rasp shut, a halting voice off-screen bawls "Smid-*large*! Mod-*wind*! Why haven't you reported for duty yet?"

A cold, uniform shiver runs up Smidlarge and Modwind's spines and they turn their heads past their shoulders to see the imposing figure of Foreman Dogel, a bullheaded and comminatory browbeater.

"You're an hour late! Just what exactly do you think you're... Oh, Ms. Cuthbertson, please do forgive me! Pardon the outburst, but these two have a history of truancy, they do."

At the mention of Ailsa's family lineage, Smidlarge and Modwind's necks swivel. A clownish note from a Harmon-muted flugelhorn carries the point across.

"W... what did you say your name was, madam?"

"It seems you're late for work, gentlemen. Now is that any kind of impression to leave on your employer?"

Smidlarge and Modwind are now in the lower-level changing rooms of Cuthbertson Industries putting on nondescript, twill one-piece uniforms, unidentifiable and featureless except for the smallest of insignias bearing the letters CI stitched on the lapels. As he is fastening his suspenders beneath his uniform, Oscar flicks Mr. Smidlarge's chest with his index and middle fingers.

"Your ship's come in, eh?"

"Not even close, Oscar. I can sniff a termagant a mile away."

"You've got her wrong, Mr. Smidlarge. Her eyes reflected a noble and gentle spirit."

"Whose side are you on, anyway? Best to get a move on before that Dogel gets back. C'mon now, hop it."

The scene transitions with breakneck speed to the two men joining a small army of other Cuthbertson maintenance workers boarding panel vans and transport trucks. Out of the back garage, a handful of vehicles pour out to various corners of the city. The A35 van on which Mr. Smidlarge and Oscar are sitting appears to be slower than the others, and is sputtering thick black smoke out of its exhaust pipe. Oscar calls out to the driver from the rear bench seat to give it more gas.

"C'mon, then! Haven't got all day!"

"Sorry, Oscar," the driver whines. "I think it might be the return line… we won't get far in this heap. Looks like you're going to have to go out on foot."

"Ahhhh-ohhhh!"

Oscar and Mr. Smidlarge carry the spirit of grim death on their faces, but beat a forsaken path to one of the Cuthbertson properties, a four-storey walk-up that sits as a perfect brick cube in a rundown part of town. The two men enter the property, and then head to a door marked *Cuthbertson Employees Only.* Inside the small, closet-sized room, there are mops and brooms on racks, a basin and a special telephone with the words *direct line* labelled on the handle. Mr. Smidlarge picks up the receiver and calls HQ. Oscar pulls out a key from around his neck that dangles from a chain. He opens a complaint box attached directly beneath the mail slot.

"Apartments six, eleven, twenty-eight and thirty-one. That's not too bad."

"Hullo, headquarters? Employee #1193 here. We're at the Waverly Heights property, confirming a work order for four apartments. Mmmhmm… are you aware of why we are behind schedule? There's hardly anything I can do about that. I see. Alright, I understand. Hmmph."

"Well, then?"

"We still have to clear all seven sites today."

"Owwhhh… It's not even possible!"

"Let's not tarry. You take the top floor and—"

"Eh? Why do I always get the top floor, Mr. Smidlarge?"

"Well, ahem, you know how my back gets, Oscar."

Sometime later, Oscar is barrelling down the stairs carrying a broom and dustpan, his face and uniform covered in soot. There is some sort of commotion coming from inside the stockroom and Oscar throws down his cleaning materials and hangs on to his cap while his feet carry him away. Two musclebound toughs are on either side of Mr. Smidlarge, shoving him about like a ragdoll. Mr. Smidlarge grimaces awkwardly as spasms of pain flutter across the lower half of his face.

"Now listen here, Smiddy, we don't want anything to happen to you. Of course we don't, do we, Eric?"

"Aye."

"So be reasonable, Smiddy. We're not asking much."

"What's all this, then?" Oscar yarps. "Let go of him!"

Oscar dives straight into the man holding up Mr. Smidlarge by the collar, but is deftly kept away by the second man, Eric. There is hardly any moving room.

"Oh, Oscar, it's you. You're with this bag of bones, then, are you? You've done right by us, but well, should we explain it to him too, Tom?"

"Occurs to us that we could do your jobs for you. Save you a spot of bother coming down here. We couldn't do that for free, though, now could we? Big job, making sure the heat don't cut out."

"You're out of your mind, you tallow-headed hooligan. Don't you listen to one word, Mr. Smidlarge. Whatever they do to us, you can be sure the boys back at headquarters will pay it back double. We, eh, eh, we know where you live, after all!"

The two extortionists consider this advice thoughtfully. Tom, the bigger of the two, lets Mr. Smidlarge fall to the ground in an ashamed heap and squeezes past Oscar. "We didn't mean anything by it, Oscar. Just messing about."

"Mr. Smidlarge, are you alright? Let's have a look at you."

Mr. Smidlarge is clutching his heart, his temples are pulsing rhythmically and he has lost his facility of speech.

"Hey! Heeey, Eric! Call an ambulance! Somebody call an ambulance!"

*   *   *

An L cut follows, and the scene shifts to Oscar at the side of Mr. Smidlarge, who is rolling in and out of consciousness in a turned-down hospital bed. Mr. Smidlarge looks up at his companion with stilled resistance in his eyes, his face in the agony that only a supposititious mortality can produce.

"Oscar, come closer…"

"Yes, Mr. Smidlarge, what is it?"

"Oscar…"

"Yes? Go on."

"You're sitting on my arm!"

Oscar bolts upright, while Mr. Smidlarge yanks his arm free from under the covers.

"Blasted hospitals, they're all the same, preparing you for the final curtain, even if you've nary begun the *second act*!"

"You gave me quite a scare, Mr. Smidlarge. How much longer do you reckon you'll be holed up in here? We've got six more jobs to finish, not to mention a trip back to Heredity and Filiation if we have the time."

"Oscar, does it look like I'll be leaving this bed any time soon?"

"But you just said—"

"Never mind what I just said. A man earns his rest as much as he earns his right to a little griping here and there."

"What did the doctor say?"

"Typical gobbledygook. Lots of bed rest, get your affairs in order…"

"Prognosis?"

"*Apparently*, I had a stroke."

"You what? Cor, that's you having me on, then! A stroke. At your ripe old age." Oscar considers his wording.

"One more and I'm finished."

"But what about what's rightfully yours then?"

"What's rightfully mine and rightfully anybody's is of no concern. They have us running around in circles while this Ailsa is getting her house in order. I didn't want to play this card but they've forced my hand. You're going to have to stand in for me, you hear? And look after Clara."

"Don't go talking nonsense."

"I have at the home, the title deed to a property on the outskirts of town—attendant documents, warranty deed—in my father's name. It's inside one of Clara's bandboxes. False bottom. I need you to go to the house and find it before Ailsa can get her mitts on it. I've left further instructions—"

"You're paranoid!"

"I've been on enough medication to sing the tune of a half million pounds, Oscar."

"Well, what am I supposed to do with it in case you've gone for a Burton by the time I come back?"

"Who's talking paranoia now, boy?"

Oscar makes shift to hurry to the Smidlarge residence. He is on his knees surrounded by twenty hatboxes that have all been upturned and discarded haphazardly in the Smidlarge bedroom. He is flinging shoes over his shoulder looking for the legal documents in question.

"Oh now, where is it?"

A shadow begins to eclipse Oscar's body from off-screen.

"Looking for something?"

Expecting Clara, Oscar rises sheepishly, but is taken aback when he sees Ailsa standing in the Smidlarges' bedroom, flanked on both sides by two boulder-headed bruisers. In Ailsa's delicate right hand is a document folded along the middle, and in the other, a bone folder and a torn manila envelope.

"How did you get in here? You're trespassing on private property! I'll notify the authorities, I will."

"I have a much more appealing proposition for you, Oscar. Why don't you come with us and let me tell you about it?"

"You must think I'm awfully gullible to fall for a nasty trick like that. I'll scream. The Smidlarges have paper-thin walls. The neighbours don't hardly leave their houses."

Ailsa divides a look of hesitation between her thugs.

"And you're in possession of stolen legal documents respecting the last will and testament of one Mr. Rewdilf Smidlarge. Felony charges, the lot of you!"

"Easy, Oscar. We were merely keeping them safe until your arrival. You know, at Cuthbertson Industries, we're all one happy family."

"Throw it here then, you pack of jackals. No tricks!"

Oscar has picked up some Christmas wrapping folded around a cardboard tube, and is brandishing it like an admiral's cutlass, stabbing it forward each time one of the burly men leans forward too suddenly.

"How about we all go on our merry way, and you can have Clara back."

Oscar is taken aback by this threat, recalling his promise to Mr. Smidlarge. He drops the tube, and the men descend upon him in seconds. He is held fast between them and escorted to a Silver Wraith waiting outside.

Type Reader: Type Books Talks with Jean Marc Ah-Sen

1) What is the first book you remember loving?

JMA: I don't know what it was called, but when I was a kid, I was obsessed with this book that explained the human body with leering automatons representing blood cells and antibodies and what not, helping its functions along: exercising, eating, getting sick. They looked like they were doing a terrible job, had been at it for donkey's years. I remember when it explained sex, the automatons were driving a tank, and with waste production, they ran this intestinal factory in a slipshod way. I was terrified, but it was a good diagnostic on life. Everybody's just barely hanging on, going through the motions, and we're just a few layers from the filth.

2) What is your favourite virtue in a book?

JMA: Probably iconoclasm, bonus if it derails the senses a bit. Not a virtue, but I'm partial to anything about subcultures, or which has a character assassination or two. Top marks if it's designed by Zak Kyes. It's a tie between those things.

3) What do you appreciate most in a book character?

JMA: World-weariness, degradation, poor posture, a cavalier attitude towards the reader.

4) What character (real or fictional) do you dislike the most?

JMA: James Bond has always annoyed me. Subtextually, a great stand-in for late capitalistic society, but otherwise it wears the adolescent male fantasy a little too liberally on its sleeve. He should be in a hospital bed reading about Gérard de Lairesse, crying himself to sleep every night. I'd read that.

5) If you were to write a non-fiction book about anything, what would it be about?

JMA: Score-settling! Most likely an unauthorized biography of someone I know.

6) Your favourite prose authors?

JMA: Keith Waterhouse, Terry Southern, Gillian Freeman, Barry Hines. Tad Friend and Graeme Wood's writing can be quite good. Joe Orton's plays rank very highly, and read prosaically I suppose.

7) Your favourite poets?

JMA: John Betjeman, the Sitwells, Shelley, Ivor Cutler, Phyllis King, Giuseppe Gioachino Belli.

8) Has a design or art book ever had an impact on your life, and if so, what was the impact?

JMA: My friend Chris gave me and my wife a copy of Marshall McLuhan and Harley Parker's *Counterblast* as a wedding present.

We all worked at a university newspaper, and the designs and types in that book somewhat informed Chris' aesthetic sense. I married my editor, so it was quite a fitting memento.

9) Do you read on public transportation?

JMA: No, not if I can help it.

10) What qualities do you want in a book you're reading while travelling?

JMA: I don't read any more when I'm abroad. I'm out and about.

11) What book have you never read but have always meant to? Do you think you will ever read it?

JMA: Before I'm forty, for sure, but I've never finished *Gargantua and Pantagruel.* I've been building myself up to it. I don't quite hate the world enough yet to be ready.

12) What book do you pretend to have read, but in fact have not?

JMA: I'm up front about what I haven't read. There's a good chance the person telling you about it hasn't read it either.

13) If you could force a single celebrity to read a specific book in its entirety, who would you choose, and what book would you make them read?

JMA: If he were alive, I'd love to have Norman Wisdom read to me from *A Child's History of England* every night. That would be a laugh.

14) What book(s) are you reading right now?

JMA: Jack London's *John Barleycorn*, Momus' *Black Letts Diary 1979* and G.V. Desani's *All About H. Hatterr*.

Notes

Beggarly Imitation is best paired with Menteurism.

The cover photograph of Kitty Collins by Ally Schmaling is reproduced here with permission.

Interior photographs sourced from the Ah-Sen, Lagacé, Bestvater and LCK archives, unless stated otherwise: Underside of Love: LCK archive; Sentiments and Directions: LCK archive; Defence of Misanthropy: Ah-Sen archive; Mahebourg: Ah-Sen archive; Ah-Sen and I: Ah-Sen archive; Sous Spectacle Cinema Research: Ah-Sen archive; Triolet: LCK archive; The Slump: Lagacé archive; Swiddenworld: Lee Henderson; Baie-du-Tombeau: LCK archive; As to Birdlime: Bestvater archive; Triolet album cover: Ah-Sen archive.

Lyrics to "Ambition" by Subway Sect used with permission from Vic Godard.

The hypomnemic paragraph structure used in this book is appropriated with esteem from the works and writing of Stephen Potter.

"Underside of Love" is loosely based on Austin Clarke's "Give Us This Day: And Forgive Us" from *When He Was Free and Young and He Used to Wear Silks*. An earlier version of this story appeared in a commemorative issue of *The Puritan* celebrating Austin Clarke's legacy. Matt Lehner and Kilworthy Tanner contributed to some of the dialogue.

The palimpsest "Ah-Sen and I" is based on the James E. Irby translation of Jorge Luis Borges' "Borges and I" published in *Labyrinths*.

A longer version of "Sous Spectacle Cinema Research Consultation with Bart Testa" originally appeared in a 2010 edition of *The Innis Herald*.

The collage "Untitled 2019" attributed to Thusnelda Baltuch was made by Lee Henderson, and is reproduced here with his permission.

The concept of the "chansons des mouches" is borrowed from Osbert Sitwell's poem of the same name published in *Wrack at Tidesend*.

The poem "X" from Behzad Molavi's *Exilian* is reproduced with permission.

The Patrick Hughes and George Brecht quotation is taken from their book *Vicious Circles and Infinity: An Anthology of Paradoxes*.

Fripperies of thought, violations of form and ropey dialogue are all desired outcomes in this miscellany.

Acknowledgements

This exercise in "birdcage lining" was sustained by—

Katrina Lagacé, Chester Lai-Lagacé and Wallace Lai-Lagacé, my web of sound.

The planetary consciousness of Grace Lai, Monique Ah-Sen, Cécile Ah-Sen, Ah-Peng, Bob Lagacé, Dolores Bestvater, Justin Lagacé, Alia Lagacé and Ivor Lagacé.

George Mantzios and Behzad Molavi, fellow auto-vulgarizers in the Age of Spleen.

Kilworthy Tanner, Naben Ruthnum, Paul Barrett, Adnan Khan, Inaam Haq, Martin Zeilinger, Christopher Heron, Robyn Thomson Kacki, James Davidson, Paul Pope, Matt Lehner, Genevieve Iacovino, Laura Briffaud, Lee Henderson, André Forget, André Babyn, Jonathan Tsao, Jason Foo, Jenn Foo, Barry Hertz, Bronwyn Dobchuk-Land, Owen Toews, Georgia Toews, Mark Boucher, Sherita Bassuday, Ranée Dong, Cory Chatwell, Rachit Chakerwarti, Kevin Fong, Pete Marino, Rick Meier, Bart Testa, Vic Godard, Ally Schmaling and Kitty Collins. With apologies to Elpenor Morien-Khalid and the White Light Technician Thinking Throne.

Silas White, Amber McMillan, Carleton Wilson and the staff at Nightwood and Harbour.

PHOTO CREDIT: JUSTIN LAGACÉ

About the Author

Jean Marc Ah-Sen is the Toronto-based author of *Grand Menteur*, which *The Globe & Mail* selected as one of the 100 Best Books of 2015. *The National Post* has hailed his work as "an inventive escape from the conventional." He lives with his wife and sons.

Listen to "Triolet" at soundcloud.com/blackderwish